Benoîte Groult was born in Paris in 1920. She studied classical philology at the Sorbonne and then taught French literature and Latin. From 1946 to 1960 she was a radio journalist. She has also been an editor at *Elle* and *Marie-Claire* and in 1978 was co-founder with Claude Servan Schreiber of *F Magazine*, a woman's journal. From 1984 until 1986 she was President of the Commission of Terminology, finding feminine forms for jobs previously reserved for men, and she has also acted as jurywoman for the Femina Prize. She is the author of six other novels, three of them written together with her sister Flora and including *Le journal à quatre mains* (*Double-Handed Diary*, 1958), the diary of two young girls during the German occupation in Paris. *Les Vaisseaux du Coeur* (1988), her most recent novel, has been first on the bestseller list in Germany for over a year. Her other publications include the biography *Pauline Roland ou un exécrable héroïsme*, a history book on Olympe de Gouges, a feminist revolutionary who was condemned to the guillotine in 1794, a translation of Dorothy Parker's *Here Lies* and an adaptation of one of Colette's novels, *Claudine à Paris*, for television. Her feminist essay *Ainsi soit-elle*, published in 1975, has been translated into fifteen languages, including Japanese and Hebrew.

Benoîte Groult is married to Paul Guimard, a journalist and writer, and has three daughters, two of them by her first marriage to a reporter, Georges de Caunes. She spends half the year in the South of France, the other half in Brittany. Apart from writing, her hobbies are sea-fishing and gardening.

BENOITE GROULT

SALT ON OUR SKIN

TRANSLATED BY
MO TEITELBAUM

PENGUIN BOOKS

PENGUIN BOOKS

Published by the Penguin Group
Penguin Books Ltd, 27 Wrights Lane, London W8 5TZ, England
Penguin Books USA Inc., 375 Hudson Street, New York, New York 10014, USA
Penguin Books Australia Ltd, Ringwood, Victoria, Australia
Penguin Books Canada Ltd, 10 Alcorn Avenue, Toronto, Ontario, Canada M4V 3B2
Penguin Books (NZ) Ltd, 182–190 Wairau Road, Auckland 10, New Zealand

Penguin Books Ltd, Registered Offices: Harmondsworth, Middlesex, England

First published in France by Bernard Grasset 1988
This translation first published in Great Britain by Hamish Hamilton Ltd 1992
Published in Penguin Books 1992
1 3 5 7 9 10 8 6 4 2

Penguin Film and TV Tie-in edition first published 1993

Copyright © Éditions Grasset et Fasquelle, 1988
This translation copyright © Mo Teitelbaum, 1992
All rights reserved

The moral right of the author and translator has been asserted

Printed in England by Clays Ltd, St Ives plc

*Truly solitary is he or she who
is nobody's number one.*

Helene Deutsch

Contents

First of All . . .

First of all, what am I going to call him so his wife never knows? A Breton name, anyway, for that's what he had. But I'd like him to have the name of a bard, one of those absurdly brave Irish heroes who lost most of their battles but never their souls.

Or a Viking name perhaps? No, the Vikings were fair-haired. Celtic rather since he so belonged to that race of sturdy dark men with light eyes and a touch of red in their beards, that people of no precise place, whose history is disputed, whose very existence is more a matter of poetry than fact.

I want it harsh and rugged to go with that solid build of his, the dark brown hair which curled low on his forehead and down his powerful neck, those vivid blue eyes which flashed like two rays of sea light beneath his bushy eyebrows, his high cheekbones and the copper-coloured beard he grew when he was at sea.

I try one name then another, turning him round before the mirror of my mind . . . This one doesn't convey his angry, obdurate look when crossed, that one doesn't match that weighty walk of his.

'Kevin'? Well, maybe, if I could be sure it would be pronounced in the English way and not 'Quévain'. 'Yves'? No, that sounds like an Icelandic fisherman, and I've come across too many 'Jean-Yves' on holiday in Brittany, all of them skinny and freckled. 'Loïc'? Possibly. But I'd like something more unique, a name for a cormorant.

How about 'Tugdual'? 'Gawain' – one of the knights of

the Round Table? Or 'Brian Boru', the Charlemagne of Ireland? But in French you pronounce it so that it means 'brilliant Boru', and the light English r, that back and forward movement of the tongue mid-palate, becomes a graceless French gargle.

And yet, to suit him truly the name must have a chivalric ring. And who more chivalrous than Gawain, son of Lot, King of Norway, and of Arthur's sister, Anne; Gawain who died in single combat with the traitor Mordred? The Arthurian stories tell us he was prudent, wise, courteous, magnanimous, of matchless prowess and unfailing loyalty to his liege lord. Not a poet, it's true, but a man eager for adventures and heroic deeds, who fulfilled his duty whatever the cost. This is the Gawain of the Breton cycle, and this is how he is, the man in my story.

In real life I thought his name silly, and, from the moment we knew each other, I made up nicknames for him. Now that all I can do is commit him to paper I dedicate this final name to him, a name beautiful to write and beautiful to read, even in the modern version: 'Gavin'.

But not without a certain apprehension do I join that band of writers who try to capture those pleasures called carnal which can get such a grip on the heart. Like many who have tried and many more, no doubt, who have given up in despair, I shall find that words don't help one express the ecstasy of love, that transport so intense that ordinary frontiers dissolve and we discover bodies we never suspected we possessed. I know I shall make myself ridiculous. I know my unique emotions will be mired in the banal and that every word, every forlorn, drab, coarse, grotesque, even frankly repellent word is waiting to betray me.

And how to write from the heart about the surgings and subsidings, dissolutions, resolutions, and resurrections of desire? What sort of emotion is evoked by the word 'coition'? *Co-ire*, the Latin for 'go together'. But when two bodies go together, what becomes of the pleasure?

Then there's 'penetration'. We're in the law courts here: 'Did penetration actually take place, Miss Smith?' 'Fornication' has a whiff of surplices and sin. 'Copulation' is ponderous, 'coupling' animal, 'sleeping with' boring and inaccurate, and 'fucking' altogether too brisk. Well then, there's 'swiving', 'tupping', 'hauchmagandy', 'quenching the fire'. These, alas, are the forgotten coinings of a youthful language, before it was bridled by sobriety. In these days of verbal inflation, when words fall out of fashion as fast as our clothes, we have only grubby obscenities rendered meaningless by constant repetition. The worthy 'making love' is always at hand, ready to serve but devoid of emotional thrill, neither scandalous nor erotic. Not fit for literature, then.

As for the organs which produce this pleasure, every writer, male or – perhaps more so – female encounters a whole new set of pitfalls: 'Jack's rod was rigid, swollen to bursting . . . Mellors' phallus raised itself, superb, awe-inspiring . . .' The assistant-director's balls, your adorable scrotum, his penis, your pubis, my vagina dentata, your clitoris, Beatrice. How to avoid becoming comic? The very science of anatomy loses its neutrality when sex comes into the picture. Words, recalcitrant bastards, insist on independent existence or impose received images on the transparency one seeks, coming as they do from slang or Latin, slime or the sublime. Where they exist at all, that is. For as far as the female orgasm is concerned, even the best writers display an appallingly meagre vocabulary.

One just has to forget everything and start afresh – forget press pornography, hard or soft, mucous membrane journalism with its relentless accounts of sexual acrobatics churned out by cynical hacks on subsistence wages. Forget more especially fashionable post-modern erotica which cloaks its nastiness in high-flown jargon.

All the same, there's no way I can tell my story without describing the sin of firkytoodling, as sexual play was known in the sixteenth century. It was by abandoning themselves to firkytoodling that my hero and heroine became enslaved to each other. It was in quest of firkytoodling that they pursued each other to the ends of the world. It was because of firkytoodling that they were never able to part, though in every other aspect of their lives they were as apart as they could be. It would be nice to say that this love came from the marriage of true minds, or a childhood bond, an extraordinary gift or a heart-rending disability of our hero or heroine. But facts had better be faced and the bare fact is, these two weren't meant to know each other, were even meant to despise each other, and it was only the speechless language of love which made them able to communicate. It was the magic of his thing in her whatsit – and perhaps a touch of the destiny one always likes to invoke in these matters, or mysterious forces or the play of hormones or whatever – which bound them so inextricably that they overcame all obstacles to their love.

What I've got to do is make the commonest act of all seem dazzling. Why write at all if you can't dazzle? So how can I describe that hope of heaven which gleams between the legs of men and women, making a miracle of an act which takes place everywhere and has done since forever, between sexes – opposite or the same – pathetically or gloriously? I'm not endowed with any special knowledge or with words which haven't been used or abused a thousand times before. This is no voyage to an undiscovered country: love has no terra incognita. In the end, there's nothing more commonplace than a cunt unless it's two cunts. When it comes to it, a phallus of the finest quality ejaculates just like any common or garden cock. Prudence would dictate giving up now. Between the pitfalls of pornography on the one hand and insipidity on the other, very few writers have scoffed at the dangers and achieved literary masterpieces that shine with an insolent brightness. But it's only after the event, once one's failed, that prudence seems such a desirable quality. Isn't all literature imprudent anyway?

But, in spite of all this, what a beautiful risk it was to write the opening lines of this impossible story: 'I was eighteen when Gavin entered my heart for life, or what I took to be my heart, though at the time it was still only my skin . . .'

1
Gavin

I was eighteen when, without either of us realising it, Gavin entered my heart for life. Yes, it began with my heart, or what I took to be my heart though, at that time, it was still only my skin. He was six or seven years older and, as a deep-sea fisherman earning his own living, he was a match for me, a middle-class student, but still dependent on my parents. My Paris friends were greenhorns and wimps beside this young man, already marked by a calling which turns a sinewy adolescent into a force of nature and, all too soon, a man old before his time. Yet boyhood still lurked in his eyes, which he dropped whenever you looked at him, and youth in the arrogant curl of his mouth. But there was a man's strength in his great hands, toughened by salt water, and his deliberate gait, each step set firmly, as if on a rolling deck.

Until we reached adolescence we eyed each other with the wariness of incompatible species – he the Breton, I the Parisienne – knowing that our paths were bound in different directions. To aggravate things, he was the son of a poor farmer and I the daughter of summer visitors. He seemed to think that being summer visitors constituted our chief occupation, a way of life for which he felt nothing but contempt. The little spare time he had was spent in violent games of football with his brothers, an activity which left me cold. Or he would shoot birds with his catapult or raid their nests, all of which revolted me. The rest of the time he would be scuffling with his mates or, if he met my sister and me, swearing like a trooper for our benefit. I decided that this was typical male behaviour, by definition hateful. It was he who punctured the tyres of my first little-rich-girl's bicycle. To be fair, that bicycle was a real kick in the teeth. All he and his brothers possessed was a clapped-out old box on wheels in which they would clatter down the one street in Raguenès, rejoicing in the racket. As soon as his legs were long enough, he flung them across his father's decrepit old nag of a pushbike and sneaked off every time the old man lay senseless in a ditch after a Saturday-night bender. My sister and I responded by using clothes-pegs to fix postcards to the wheels of our shiny chrome bicycles, with their bells and mudguards and their little baskets. This made a whirring engine-like noise which was meant to impress the Lozerech boys. They took no notice whatsoever.

There was a sort of tacit agreement that we play with the one girl of the Lozerech family, the youngest of what my father dismissively described as 'that brood of rabbits'. She was a charmless little blonde, with a name, Yvonne, which we thought lamentable. As I said, we had nothing in common.

When he was fourteen or fifteen Gavin disappeared from my horizon. He was already at sea during the summer as ship's boy on his brother's trawler, the *Vaillant Couturier*. I was charmed by the name: for a long time I believed it was for a real valiant couturier, renowned for some unexpected act of bravery at sea. Gavin's mother used to say that he wasn't one to shirk and it wouldn't be long before his apprenticeship was over. But for the moment he was just ship's boy, the scapegoat on board. That was the custom and a skipper had less right to be soft with a relative than others.

For my sister and me this simply meant one enemy fewer in the village. But the five remaining Lozerech boys continued to consider us as useless because we were girls and stuck-up because we came from Paris. This was made even worse by the fact that my name was George. 'George without an s, as in George Sand,' my mother would proclaim, having sacrificed me on the altar of her youthful passion for *Indiana*. My younger sister, who had been less controversially christened Frédérique, scolded me for being ashamed. I retaliated by calling her 'Frédéric with a q-u-e'. I would have given much not to suffer the teasing and questions at the start of each school year, before the new ones got used to it. Children are merciless to anyone who doesn't conform, and I was well into adulthood before I forgave my mother. It wasn't such a problem at my college, Sainte-Marie, as in the country. At least people there recognised the name, even if it was devoid of the odour of sanctity. But in any case, by the end of her life, George Sand had redeemed herself with a couple of pious novels, and by becoming the good Lady of Nohant. But at Raguenès my name furnished an inexhaustible source of mockery. They never tired of it; the target was irresistible.

It did not help that, instead of being among all the other holiday homes, our house was in the middle of a working village, inhabited only by fishermen and farmers. We stuck out like the proverbial sore thumb. The 'beachwear' sported by my mother and the vast berets and tweed plus-fours which my father affected caused constant hilarity. The village boys kept quiet if our parents were around, but if they caught us alone they were transformed into a pack of male animals, flaunting the superiority supposedly endowed by their willies, and taking every opportunity, the minute they spotted us in the distance, to scoff at my sister and me. Gavin in the lead, they would bray stupid doggerel. The sillier they got the more furious we became.

Parisiennes,
Silly hens!
From the town,
Silly clowns!

When you're a child, the silliest jokes are often the best ones. We got our revenge when we encountered our tormentors singly or in pairs. In a group they were Man. Isolated they were just one kid against another; or worse, a farm boy faced with a city girl.

Gavin had never been to our house. He didn't think it was a house anyway, but a pretentious villa with a ridiculous thatched roof. For the villagers real roofs were made of slate. Our meticulously authentic thatch of hand-beaten rye-straw, hard to find and costing the earth from the last thatcher in the district, seemed to be flying in the face of common sense. So to say something as ordinary as 'Come round to our place for tea' or, later, 'Come in for a drink', was out of the question. It was different with Yvonne. She was my age, and I often asked her to play at our house. We, of course, could turn up at the farm whenever we felt like it. To Frédérique and me, from our pristine house where we had to tidy our toys and blanco our canvas sandals every day, the farm seemed the height of freedom. There was always something going on, the mess of eight children's clothes all over the place, and rows of muddy clogs by the back door. The farm-yard was over-run with cats and dogs and chickens, and cluttered with rickety rabbit hutches and implements of inde-terminate use which looked decrepit but would nevertheless, once a year, be indispensable for some task or other. These visits were always one way, as in those nineteenth-century tales where the lady of the manor and her daughters called on the sick and the deserving poor – grateful tenants who would never dream of visiting the big house. Sometimes, after lifting potatoes with Yvonne – an unattractive job if ever there was one, but one which I did in the hope that it would make me look less of a feeble townee – I stayed to eat with the Lozerechs. There, the bacon soup I would have detested at home seemed delicious, and I was prouder of being able to milk a cow than I was of my high grades at school. I liked to think that in another life I might have made a good farm girl.

It was harvest time when Gavin and I first saw each other as human beings rather than representatives of hostile social groups. At threshing time everyone lent a hand, and families would try to assemble as many people as possible before starting. Three of the Lozerech sons, including Gavin, were at home at the same time, and the family made the most of the opportunity to fix the date for the big job ahead. Naturally, as immediate neighbours, Frédérique and I helped every year, and we were proud of sharing the work, the exhaustion at the end of the day, and the excitement of the most important event of the year, one which determined the annual income of the whole household.

The last day had been stifling. On the two preceding days we had gathered in the barley and oats, and now it was time for the wheat. The air shimmered with the heat and a fine choking dust which got into our eyes and throats, and throbbed with the noise of the threshing machine. The dust powdered the hair and head-dresses of the women and turned their dark skirts grey, while streams of dark sweat trickled down the faces and necks of the men. Only Gavin worked bare-chested. Standing on top of the cart, he slashed the twine which bound the sheaves with one stroke of his sickle, then straddled the sheaves and swung them on to the conveyor belt in a gesture I thought magnificent. The sheaves bounced their way down the belt. He gleamed with fine young sweat in the sunlight, the golden wheat flying all around him, while his muscles played ceaselessly under his skin, like the shining muscled quarters of the great horses which periodically brought fresh loads of sheaves.

I had never seen a man so manly except in Hollywood movies, and I was proud to be a participant at this annual ritual. To be, for once, part of his world. I loved everything about those sultry days: the intensity, the smoking bags of wheat with their acrid smell – symbols of abundance filled under the eagle eye of Gavin's father who made sure that not a grain of his treasure was lost – and the three o'clock tea: a banquet of fat bacon, pâté and deep yellow butter spread thickly on chunks of bread, which made our Parisian tea times seem bloodless affairs. I even loved the men swearing every time the belt slipped and had to be levered back on to the pulleys, while everyone else seized the chance to slake their parched throats with a pull of cider. And how marvellous it was when all the sacks were heaped in the barn ready for the mill, and the *fest noz*, for which they always slaughtered and roasted a pig, could begin.

That evening everyone sprawled around, drunk with exhaustion. United by work well done, a harvest safely in, we basked in a late July dusk which seemed reluctant to yield to darkness. At that time of year in Brittany the long twilights linger on, giving the illusory hope that, just this once, day will conquer night. I was sitting next to Gavin, weak with pleasure at being so near him but utterly tongue-tied. At least I knew better than to go into raptures about nature with country people, but having grown out of the games and battles of childhood, we had nothing to put in their place and were silent, constrained by our age. The Lozerech boys and Gallois girls were retreating into their respective social classes after the no-man's-land of childhood. Soon, when we met, we would be reduced to nods and smiles, having nothing to say, not even the old taunts. Oh, we'd still be 'friends' of course, still ask after each other's lives – 'How's the catch these days?' 'Exams going OK then?' – but the answers would be treated absent-mindedly, like shells you don't bother to gather on a winter beach.

But now, this evening, hovering between day and night, between dream and reality . . . As the party was about to break up Gavin, in spite of the tiredness softening his features, suddenly suggested driving over to Concarneau. No one was keen to begin with; they just wanted to fall into bed. But then another Lozerech boy came round to the idea and using all the persuasive tactics at my disposal, I implored Yvonne to join us, pledging my best lacy bra, my most expensive toilet water, anything so as not to be the only girl. Gavin was one of the few people in the village who had a car, an old 4CV, and he piled in as many people as it could hold. Frédérique stayed behind: a fifteen-year-old simply doesn't go dancing in Concarneau.

For a girl who had only been to faculty balls the affair at the Ty Chupenn Gwen hotel was as exotic as an Apache war dance. Luckily Yvonne took me under her wing. I was very much the outsider in this crowd of rowdy young men already the worse for drink, but at least I wouldn't be the wallflower I was in Paris, too often reduced to hiding behind the record player. As soon as we arrived Gavin drew me on to the dance floor without a word and, before anyone else had a chance, settled me in his arms as firmly as he would grasp a trawler-stay. I was aware of each finger of the hand on my ribs.

Proper hands, I told myself. They wouldn't let you fall, not like the pale, distinguished hands waved around by the pale, distinguished young men I knew in Paris. He danced like a man of the people, like one of Zola's workers, with a swing of the shoulders pronounced enough to seem common to my bourgeois code of etiquette. Not once did his eyes meet mine and neither of us said a word. He wouldn't have known what to say and I couldn't think of a single subject of conversation. 'Do you like Rilke's *Letters to a Young Poet*?' (even I knew that wouldn't do) or, 'How's the fishing going?' (that wouldn't do either). What does a student of classics and history say to a young man who spends most of his time on a trawler on the Irish Sea? I stayed speechless, dumb with shyness and the unexpected sensation of being in Gavin's arms. But it didn't matter, since he kept his arms round me between dances, waiting for the music to begin again. He still smelled of sunshine and wheat, and I thought he handled me with the same serious concentration he had given the sheaves earlier that day. In any case, what words could have expressed the absurd, incongruous feeling of recognition between our bodies, the sense that our souls – for it certainly wasn't our minds – were striving towards each other, regardless of worldly obstacles. Naturally Plato came into my head. At that age I channelled all my thoughts and emotions through the words of poets and philosophers. And Gavin had recklessly surrendered to the same spell. I was sure of it somehow, sure that feelings like these are always mutual. The spell held through a waltz and two *paso doble*s and swung us along in a sultry tango, while reality blurred and receded. The voices of the Raguenès boys reached me as if from a distant planet. They were getting noisier and more facetious to hide their growing lust for the girls they were trying to soften up with drink and hopeful fumbling. When the lights suddenly went out Gavin and I found ourselves outside by silent accord. Selfish with happiness, we decided that Yvonne and the others could find their own way home, and, like a pair of cowards, drove off in the 4CV.

He took the road to the sea, of course. You head for the sea instinctively at times like this. The sea absolves any need for talk. It enfolds you like a mother, wraps you in indulgent silence. But we were checked at le Cabellou, la Dument, Trévignon and the beach at Raguenès. There was no through road along the coast then, only dead ends, emblematic of our own situation. The less we spoke, the more the silence swelled. Gavin kept his arm round my shoulders, brushing my cheek with his temple now and again.

At Raguenès the tide was out. The spit of sand which joined the island to the shore at low water shone in the moon-light. To the east, where there was shelter from the prevailing wind, we could just make out the line where the sea met the sand. It was smooth as glass. To the west a breath of wind ruffled the silver expanse with its frilled, phosphorescent edge. It was still, so pure, so like us. We got out of the car to walk in that silent water.

'Why don't we take a midnight swim?' The notion came to me all at once. It was the first time we had ever been by the sea together. In those days Bretons hardly ever went to the beach; swimming was a crack-brained trippers' fancy. Sailors and fishermen, they had gone down at sea too often, for too many centuries, to think of it as a place for fun and games.

We undressed at a discreet distance from each other, careful not to look. I had never taken my clothes off in front of a boy before but that didn't stop me feeling disappointed that

Gavin didn't even glance at me. I was beautiful in the moonlight, I felt sure, less truly naked than in the glare of electric light. As much to hide my 'front' as to avoid looking at his, I raced into the sea first, joyously splintering the bright mirror. I didn't go far. Almost immediately I guessed that Gavin couldn't swim. 'What's the point? Only makes it worse if you're swept overboard at night in a freezing sea.' I realised then that Gavin's sea was a different person from mine, and that he knew the real one.

We played around in the icy water for ages, laughing and brushing together like a pair of happy whales, delaying the moment when we would have to get out. On dry land we knew we would don our social differences along with our clothes. It was one of those unreal nights when a sort of phosphorescent plankton comes to the surface, when each stroke, each splash causes luminous ripples, and sends sparks flashing into the darkness. A wave of sudden sadness engulfed us, quite disproportionate to the transitoriness of that moment: it was as if we had experienced a lifelong passion and were about to be separated by something as inexorable as war. That something was dawn, as it happened. The sky was lightening in the east, bringing the world back to its rightful proportions.

Gavin dropped me off at my door. A light was still on in my mother's room. He kept a respectful distance as he said in his normal voice, 'Well, 'bye then.' And after a pause, more softly, 'See you again, maybe.' I replied just as flatly, my arms clamped to my sides, 'Thanks for bringing me home.' As if he could have done anything else! Our houses were next door to each other.

Two days later he was to rejoin his *Vaillant Couturier*, and I wouldn't see him again that summer. My family and I were due back in Paris in September. How is it possible to imagine life on the winter seas from the warmth of a city room? What sort of gang-plank can be thrown between the deck of a trawler and the lecture theatre where my professor analysed the protocols of courtly love?

Gavin's car set off towards the farm and was soon swallowed up by darkness. I went inside, shaking my wet hair. Saying goodnight to my mother robbed the occasion of all its romance. Everything I had lived that night started to slip away, to vanish like those dreams which fade so fast as you wake no matter how hard you try to hold on to them. But, till the very end of that summer, I felt that my steps faltered a little, that a fine mist lay over my blue eyes.

These feelings came to a head on one of those soft Breton evenings which mark the turn of season, and became a poem, a sort of message in a bottle for Gavin which I didn't dare throw in the sea for fear of ridicule. What would his friends say? With them he might snigger at the qualms of the city girl. 'You know, them that has the thatched house at the end of the village . . .' 'The daughter's not bad . . .' 'Nah. D'you reckon?' These fears prevented my sending Gavin the poem, the first love poem of my life.

> So innocent, by the ocean,
> So innocent, we two.
> You a child-man, diffident,
> Who would never read Gide.
> And I cold as the first woman,
> In the night as tender as night.
>
> We halted on the brink of time,
> At the brink of passion.
> You a man, I still a girl,

But rigidly calm, controlled –
A pose one's disposed to at eighteen.

Often I return to Raguenès,
I who have read Gide,
To recapture your fleeting eyes
And the trembling fierceness of your mouth.
Today I am tender as the first woman,
But the nights are as cold as night.

If I could but kiss you now,
With the taste of salt on our skin,
You who sail the Irish Sea,
Who ride the bucking waves,
Away from my twenty years,
Away from the sweet shore,
Where you took me to find the fabulous beast,
Which never did appear.

And you?
Do you ever return to that meeting-place,
To lament the love we never made?

Soon it was time to shut the house up for another winter, to leave my eighteenth summer behind. I abandoned the poem to my weed garden holiday clutter in a drawer, together with a bronze kirby-grip still fastened to its yellowing card, a pink sea urchin shell, a solitary sock whose pair might yet turn up, an ear of corn I'd hoarded from that evening of harvest. When we returned the next summer I didn't throw the poem away. I still hoped it might reach its addressee one day and recall to him the unforgettable taste of first desire.

2
Yvonne's Wedding

It was two years before I saw Gavin again. He had chosen the sea as his work for good and become second mate, which meant he was never in Raguenès for more than a couple of days every fortnight, waiting on the tide. In the autumn he planned to go to the Maritime College at Concarneau to study for a captain's certificate. He had mapped out his life on predictable lines. For instance, he'd just got engaged, 'because a bloke can't live with his parents for ever'. At least that's what he said to me, as if excusing himself. His fiancée, Marie-Josée, worked in a Concarneau factory. They weren't in any hurry, he said. They still had to build themselves a house at Larmor, on a plot of land left to him by his grandmother. They had mortgaged themselves for twenty years even before the first stone was laid. He and I avoided one another, not wanting to seem stand-offish or to hurt each other's feelings. Or, it should be said, he avoided me. While, if we did meet, I quite liked making that gorgeous young man lower his eyes. On the other hand, if I ever met him in a shop he would lapse into broad Breton, just to show me I didn't belong.

It was at Yvonne's wedding that he was compelled to look me in the eyes again. She had insisted on my being her witness, while Gavin had promised to be the groom's witness. The groom was a sailor too, but in the Navy rather than a fisherman. Yvonne had been determined to marry away from the land. She loathed it. She loathed looking after the farm animals, she loathed the permanently chapped, red hands in winter, the clogs caked with mud even on Sundays, the whole relentless rhythm of farm life. But she knew she didn't want an offshore trawlerman, a homebound creature like her brother Robert, who was there every evening, his hands reeking of bait, and who woke her at four in the morning when he went out to sea. Nor did she fancy a long-distance trawlerman like two of her other brothers. No, what she was after was someone who barely knew what a fish looked like, someone with a uniform, someone, above all, who would be away for months on end – months which would count double for his pension. She had already worked that one out. He should be able to give her the chance of a year or two in Djibouti, Martinique or even, if she got lucky, Tahiti. And the rest of the time she would have her nice little house. And peace. Peace was Yvonne's real goal. For the whole of her life so far she had scarcely been allowed to sit down except at meals. And even then she and her mother would be constantly up and down, waiting on seven boys and the father and the gormless yokel who was their only farm hand. Every time Yvonne pronounced the word 'peace' she had an ecstatic smile on her face. Peace was never again having to scurry to endless shouts of 'Yvonne, where's the bloody cider? We haven't got all day,' or 'Yvonne, get yourself down to the wash house! Your brother can't go off without clean clothes,' or 'Yvonne! Stop dreaming. The cow can't calve on her own.' Marriage seemed to offer a haven of tranquillity and she grabbed the first man who fitted the bill. The fact that he was a weedy specimen didn't seem to worry her in the slightest. He was so short he had needed special dispensation to join the Navy – short in the head as the local backbiters put it. None the worse for that: she would find his absences easier to bear.

The difficulty was finding a date for the wedding. It had

to be a time when all three seafaring brothers were at home, trickier now that they were all on different ships. It had to fit in with the holidays of the brother who was a teacher at Nantes, and with my own time in Raguenès. Yvonne was the Lozerechs' only daughter, and they were bent on a grand wedding, with three bridesmaids all rigged out in almond-green organza and guests ferried in by coach from all over south Finistère.

And I meant it to be a grand wedding for Gavin and me too. Celebrations seemed fated to be our downfall. Indeed, we were side by side at nine o'clock in the morning, sipping our first glass of muscadet, and I knew we should have to be more or less together the whole day, part of the night, and again the following day for the traditional 'bringing back the bride'. Gavin looked like a performing bear, almost unrecognisable, in his Sunday best, his unruly curls glued down with some sort of hair-cream. I knew I was maddeningly cool and elegant, very much the sophisticated Parisienne in a manifestly expensive creation of palest beige wild silk and matching ankle-strap shoes which made my naturally good legs look even better, and had that air of unruffled self-assurance, the privilege of everyone who has never dreamed of being born elsewhere than in the soft cradle accorded them by fate. That morning I was the embodiment of everything that Gavin most hated. It simply made me more determined to crack that tough shell of his and get to the vulnerable core which I was certain lay within. That night on the beach lingered in my mind, like a door too quickly slammed on a barely glimpsed vista of light. Could I have imagined those feelings which still had the power to pierce my heart? And had Gavin felt them too? Had I been mistaken about the intensity of his mood that night? I certainly wasn't going to spend the rest of my life in frustrated nostalgia. I would get to the truth that day if it killed me.

There was nothing to be done while we hung around interminably for photographs in front of the tiny chapel in Saint-Philibert, where the weedy specimen had been born. A spiteful breeze fluttered the bonnet ribbons and the Breton ruffs worn by the mothers of the bride and groom and a few other diehard traditionalists. Another gust made my exquisitely set 'natural' curls droop round my face in limp hanks.

When at last the photographer folded his tripod and covered his camera with a baize cloth we all trooped off to the Café du Bourg for drinks and dancing. But as soon as we got in, the men all clustered round the bar and the lads round the pinball machines, leaving the women to their own concerns. It was two o'clock in the afternoon before I found myself next to Gavin at the top table. He was already a bit drunk but it was clear that the poor innocent was all set to work his way through the muscadet, the bordeaux, the champagne and the liqueurs which are obligatory at affairs like these. Mind you, I was counting on this for Operation Truth. Even before the inevitable ox tongue in madeira sauce, which would mean changing from white wine to red, I was acutely aware of Gavin's body, so close to mine. My father always quoted, 'White on red, clear head. Red on white wrecks your night'. He ignored me completely. I told myself that it was because his fiancée was on the other side, looking prim in a pink dress which swore at her sallow complexion and the not-quite-blonde-enough hair, frizzed into one of those desiccated perms all the rage in Concarneau. She paraded a Queen of England bosom, a sort of single breast slung across her front like a bolster. Poor Gavin, I thought, having to settle for that cushiony bulge. The wine was getting to me and I longed wistfully to feel his hand, both hands, on my breasts, soon, before the day was out. But how to make it happen? I concocted approaches so crude that he would have had to be even cruder to resist them – my sensitive soul could wait to reveal itself later. But like all the improper gestures I've ever thought of making in my life, the one that would have roused Gavin from his irritating indifference escaped me. My body is obviously better brought up than my imagination.

As the hours passed, Yvonne's wedding-feast slowly ran out of steam. Everyone sank into torpid repletion among the crumbs and stains and overturned glasses. Under the table the farmers' wives undid their belts and kicked off the clumping court shoes bought from market stalls which had tortured their feet all day. Men queued for the lavatories and returned with expressions of relief, still buttoning their flies. Over-excited children tore around, screaming and knocking chairs over. The bridegroom was guffawing with his mates, to show he had the situation well in hand. And poor Yvonne, rather red of nose and shiny of complexion under the head-dress of florist's roses, was making her acquaintance with the loneliness of young wives.

I bided my time, sure my opportunity would come with the dancing. But we weren't there yet by any means. The party got a new lease of life with the arrival of the wedding cake and champagne, which gave the green light for a sing-song. A handful of old men, voices quavering as much with booze as decrepitude, were bent on subjecting us to every single verse of those endless Breton ballads about partings and broken promises and watery graves which paint such a tempting picture of the future for young seamen's wives. Then a woman who fancied herself as a chanteuse embarked on a popular song of the time, and didn't quite manage to massacre it. We must have got to the seventh chorus when Gavin suddenly stood up to enthusiastic applause and launched into 'Bro Goz Va Zadou'. His voice bowled me over; not that it would have taken much. It was a fine bass, which resonated on the harsh, heartrending Breton syllables. That bard's voice, combined with his touching assurance, went so well with his massive chest and those shoulder muscles which bulged, almost indecently, under his skimpy jacket. The Trégunc tailor insisted on encasing these hulking men in skin-tight suits which clung to their backsides and strained over their great thighs.

It was Marie-Josée who gave the green light for kissing Gavin when he got to the chorus:

> The parish priest gets mad
> When boys go kissing girls,
> But turns out quite a lad
> When boys get kissed by girls.

Well, who was I to pass up a chance to kiss the boy Lozerech? And it wasn't going to be just a peck, either. I waited until last, so as not to join the bleating herd of women queueing up for handsome Gavin's lips. He was laughing loudly, flushed with success, revealing the chipped front tooth which gave him a buccaneering air, as appealing as a pirate's patch. I was right next to him so all I had to do was lean across and plant a quick kiss on that front tooth, as if by accident.

He shot me a look. No, he hadn't forgotten that night on the beach. But we still had to endure the ritual of drinking sangria at the Café du Port while everyone waited for the local stars – the Daniel Fabrice band from Melgven – who were booked for the dancing. Now I was sure, though, that my hour would soon come.

The ballroom was ghastly: bare and harshly lit, and I caught sight of myself in a mirror and saw that the long day had done nothing for my looks. To make matters worse, a whole new gang of guests arrived, some of them summer visitors, friends of mine. They pranced in fresh as paint, looking about them as if they were at the zoo. Of course, I was drawn into their orbit. It was mine too, after all. I kept casting desperate glances at Gavin – to no avail. I might just as well not have been there at all. I experimented with all the tried and tested techniques: staring mesmerically at the back of his head, being wildly vivacious when I thought he might be looking my way, ostentatiously refusing to dance even the tangos, roaming the room like a lost soul. But none of my ploys worked. It was Marie-Josée whom Gavin took in his arms for all my favourite dances.

Oh well, nothing to do but rejoin my own kind and forget the handsome peasant. No hope left for me here. The party was pathetic. Everything was pointless. It had all turned out for the best, no doubt. What would I have done with Gavin afterwards? He would only have been hurt. My wounded pride soothed itself with these lofty sentiments.

Yvonne's father was surprised when I went to take my leave. 'You're not staying for the onion soup?' I most certainly was not. I couldn't stand the sight of Gavin and his bodyguard a moment longer. Suddenly I felt tired and a thousand miles away from the whole Lozerech clan. I kissed Yvonne quickly, and slipped away with my friends. Frédérique was all sweet reason: 'You'd only have spoiled a beautiful memory.' That made me even crosser. Who wants beautiful memories? I hate them. What *I* like is beautiful prospects.

Outside the hotel, I picked my way through the bodies

lying all over the garden. Some still twitched, crooning bits of songs or raising a limp arm heavenwards to emphasise drunken pronouncements. Suddenly I was startled by a hand on my shoulder.

'I've got to see you.' Gavin's whisper was harsh. 'Wait for me by the harbour. I'll be with you as soon as I can. By one at the latest.'

It wasn't a question and he didn't wait for an answer. His friends called him and Frédérique was waiting impatiently in the car. But I took my time. As I allowed the meaning of his words to sink in I drew a deep breath and a wave of happiness broke over me, filling me with blazing, joyous resolution.

After the smoky dance hall the west wind blew the smell of seaweed and of sex. I went home, to establish an alibi with my parents and to collect my duffle-coat so it could cushion me on the hard ground under Gavin's one hundred and sixty-five or so pounds. Just in case, I grabbed the poem, the one I'd written two years earlier. Before I left I showed it to Frédérique. She pulled a face and said it was terribly school-girlish. I thought it was beautiful myself. You always get a bit schoolgirlish when you're racing off to be loved, don't you?

There was no moon. The Isle of Raguenès could just be seen, a darker mass on the dark sea. Everything seemed poised in stillness, as if waiting for something. Correction: I was waiting for something. For nature it was a summer night like any other. From the moment I got there I was caught up in the exquisite state of passionate anticipation, aware that this was the highest experience life can offer. That evening I would gladly have sacrificed ten years of my life – well, five anyway – to ensure that nothing would now come between us and the drama we were about to play, though neither of us yet knew our lines. What are a few years of old age when you're twenty? I was preparing for a night with no tomorrow – outside convention, outside caution, outside even hope. I felt such wild joy.

At last he arrived. His car stopped at the top of the cliff and I heard the door slam. I could just make him out as he peered around in the darkness. He must have glimpsed me in the headlights because he started running down the rocky slope. I was sitting with my back against a beached dinghy, sheltering from the wind, clasping my arms around my knees trying to look alluring and casual at the same time. One tends to strike poses at twenty.

Before I could say a word he took my hands and pulled me up to him, clasping me fiercely, his leg thrusting between mine and his mouth forcing my lips apart. My tongue caught on that chipped tooth and, for the first time, I reached my hand under his coat, into the warm odour of him, my fingers, under his belt, finding that touching hollow of his back where the muscles flexed and twisted.

A silent rain began to fall. Neither of us noticed at first. We were in another world. For a moment I thought he must be crying, and drew back to search his eyes. His hair was falling in shining curls on his forehead, and drops sparkled on his eyelashes. Perhaps they were tears after all. Our lips came together again, parted for a breath and then joined, slippery with the delicious taste of summer rain. The dark air, the melancholy stretch of wet sand, the sea, pocked with rain, all surrounded and distanced us from the hot busy day, plunging us into the almost unbearable simplicities of love.

The rain was beginning to work its way under our collars, and the south-westerly breeze was getting stronger. But it felt as if we would never again be able to let each other go. With a jerk of his chin Gavin indicated the cottage on the island. It was a ruin, with just one section of the roof held up by a single beam. I smiled: we had played there throughout our childhood.

'We'll make it,' he said. 'The tide'll be out till about two.'

We ran across the sand bank which links the island to the shore at low tide. I twisted my ankle on a clump of seaweed but Gavin, who could see in the dark with those husky-dog eyes of his, pulled me up on to the ridge of grass in front of our cottage or what was left of it. We stood there, out of breath, our hands still clasped together, grave with the thrill of wanting so much what we were about to do together, in that place, without a thought of the past or what was to follow. Perhaps the moment of greatest, most intense joy is that one, when everything life has to offer comes together and you forget the rest.

We made for the only dry corner on the beaten earth floor of our ruin. I congratulated myself on thinking of the dufflecoat. I found myself babbling, 'It's you? Tell me you're really here. I can't be sure in this dark . . .' And he murmured, 'I knew we'd find each other again some day, I knew it,' stroking my face as if he were seeing it with his fingers, before gently exploring the back of my neck, my shoulders, my waist, sculpting me bit by bit in the exquisite clay of expectancy.

No one could have described me as experienced. At twenty I had had only two lovers: Gilles, who 'initiated' me – into precisely nothing, given that neither of us really knew what to put where; and Roger, whose intelligence rendered me speechless with admiration and incapable of judgment. He would despatch me briskly between physics lectures on the

Moroccan rug in his bed-sit ('facilities on the landing') with four or five quick bumpety-bumps preceded by about the same number of rubbedy-dubs for starters. I'm reminded of it, in spite of myself, every time I see a violinist plucking a string with the tip of his middle finger and then releasing it once he's got, or thinks he's got, the desired effect. He would manage a few considerate *I love yous* and I would respond 'I love you', mainly to convince myself that there really was something special about that quarter of an hour. I looked forward to it hopefully every time, though it must have been obvious that I never achieved even his rudimentary satisfaction. But it didn't seem to bother him, and he wanted me the next time, so I must be OK, and this must be physical love (as I called it then). I liked the before part, he preferred the after – perhaps the well-known difference between the sexes lay there.

I don't remember if Gavin was as good a caresser then as he became later. In those days men like him didn't go in much for caressing, nor would I have been for it. I assumed that Roger's approach was standard. Women who were brazen enough to ask, 'A bit higher please,' or 'No, not there, it hurts,' or even worse, 'More of that, please,' were insatiable harpies who drove good men to nice girls, girls content to worship their magic wand and drink their sacred semen with first-communion expressions. That was the received wisdom then, and anyway I had no way of checking. There was little frankness between men and women; we simply didn't speak the same language. One belongs to one's sex as to one's race.

All the barriers came down that first time. It was as if our bodies had known each other for ever: matching passion, matching rhythms carried us across every difference that had divided us, as if our whole lives had been a preparation for this love-making, this losing of ourselves in each other, this never-ending desire. As one wave of pleasure ebbed, the ripples of the next one stirred. We were living a night without time, of which there are so few in a lifetime.

It was the tide which recalled us. Gavin could suddenly tell from the sound of the waves that they were rising. That man always knew exactly what the sea was up to. 'If we don't leave now we'll have to swim for it.'

We scrabbled blindly for our scattered garments. My bra had vanished. Too bad. It didn't have my name on it, after all. Gavin swore as he fumbled with his wet buttonholes, but eventually we were dressed, more or less, me with my stupid handbag over my arm as if I were off to a tea party, and Gavin with his trousers slung round his neck so they wouldn't get wet in the sea, even though they were already soaked by the rain. Hardly able to control our laughter, we ran splashing towards the narrows through which a strong current was already coursing. We clung together to avoid being swept away and, waist deep, just managed to ford across. How better to wash oneself of love?

Gavin's car seemed so cosy and dry, as we struggled with our sopping clothes. Back at the village he parked in the farmyard to walk me home past the warmth of the cowshed where you could hear the animals stirring in the straw. We could have done with that warmth ourselves, but it was time to return to our normal lives. Chilled suddenly, we took refuge in our last kiss.

'I've got something for you,' I whispered. I took out my poem, thoroughly damp by now. 'You'll think it's very silly, probably, but I wrote it after . . . you know, that night . . . two years ago . . .'

'You felt it as well, then?' Gavin was speaking in his darkness voice. 'I thought . . .'

'It's you who never let on!'

'It was better not . . . for both of us, I reckoned. Tonight I never meant . . . I just couldn't resist it. And now I could kick myself. I'm a right bastard.'

'Why? Because you're engaged?'

He shrugged. 'It was because of you I got engaged. I mean, to stop myself getting ideas. It couldn't work for us from the start. I never thought it could. I shouldn't have asked you tonight. It was bloody stupid of me. I'm sorry.'

He rested his head with its tight ram's curls on my shoulder, breathing hard. I longed to tell him that he would have been more stupid if he hadn't. I knew already that you don't get many chances like that. But he wouldn't have understood. He didn't function along those lines. And anyway the rain came down harder, my duffle-coat smelt like a wet dog, the mud was seeping into our shoes and we were shivering with cold and sadness. In his case, with anger too at having surrendered to his feelings. This wasn't at all how he'd planned his life. I could feel him flexing, impatient to get back to the certainties of his ordered life.

'I'll forgive you,' I said. 'On condition that we meet just once again before you start at Concarneau this winter. Only once. But a proper bed, and no tide coming in. I'd like to know you better before I forget you.' Gavin's arms tightened round me. He wouldn't forget me now. He couldn't.

'*Va Karedig*,' he breathed. 'I wouldn't dare call you that in French. Lucky it's dark . . . I can't promise. I don't know. But I want you to know that . . .'

He stopped. I knew what he wanted me to know. Here he was, a trawlerman, engaged to be married, full of scruples

37

and complexes, wanting to do the right thing. Meanwhile, I wanted to stay unforgettable, even if it meant wrecking his marriage. That is the lucid cruelty that girls have. Not for a second did I feel it might be better for him to be at peace in another woman's arms. I needed the subtle joy of instilling in him an incurable nostalgia.

'*Kenavo . . . A Wechall*,' he added, even more softly, drawing away. Then in the rough Breton accent I loved so much, which swallowed the ends of his words, 'I'll do what I can about meeting again.' He raised his right hand, as if on oath, and held it there until I shut our front door behind me.

3
Paris

The great experiences of life, birth, illness, death, so often reduce one to utter banality. It's the platitudes, born of accepted wisdom which work for gut feelings, rather than any scholarly language. When Gavin kept his promise and joined me in Paris I found myself unable to sleep or eat. I was weak at the knees, had a lump in my throat, a knot in my stomach and a weight in my heart. It was as if every function had been subsumed in sexuality. And those weren't the only parts of me aflame: a fire raged at my core for three days, a brand from Gavin's red-hot iron. Like that vaginal ring in *The Story of O*.

'You'll never imagine where, but I'm on fire,' I told him, not quite daring to be explicit. We didn't know each other very well after all.

'I can imagine where, never stop imagining it,' he answered with a village boy look, torn between being pleased at this homage to his virility and shocked at the plain speaking he didn't expect from someone with my education. I enjoyed shocking him. It was so easy to do. His own world was rigid, with people and things allotted watertight compartments where they were supposed to stay.

As I smoothed a soothing ointment over the afflicted area I wondered why the authors of erotic books never mentioned these minor accidents of pleasure. Their heroines have cast-iron vaginas, endlessly receptive to the intrusion of foreign bodies. Mine felt flayed. In the magnifying mirror I could scarcely recognise my neat, distinguished vulva. In its place was an inflamed apricot, swollen, rudely bursting from its usual confines, in short utterly indecent and incapable of admitting so much as a piece of spaghetti. And yet it wasn't long before I was accepting, indeed imploring, his branding iron, begging him to penetrate me once more with that enormous thing. And, against all physical laws, the first searing pain over, it fitted perfectly, like a glove as one says. Any other time, I should have pleaded for a truce, but there was so little time now. Against expectations, having counted on filling up my tank and going off happily, I found myself wanting him more and more. Being beside him constantly, breathing his wheaten smell, stunned by perpetual desire, absorbed all my faculties. I lay awake at night, nourishing myself with his proximity while he slept. By day, I fed on his handsomeness, the caress of those hands which looked so hard and rough but had a goldsmith's delicacy when they touched me.

Occasionally, a bit ashamed of ourselves, we tried to restrain our animal frenzy by going to see the Eiffel Tower, the Arc de Triomphe, the Louvre. Making the tourist rounds instead of love. As it was his first visit to Paris I took Gavin on a *bâteau mouche*. But all our sight-seeing trips were cut short. Clinging together, aching with desire, we pretended to stroll around, like normal people. But he had only to let his glance linger on my breasts or brush my leg with his powerful thigh or look at me in a way that had nothing to do with the façade of the Louvre and we'd race back to the hotel room, guilty at our haste but unable to hide it.

Or we plunged into a bar. Only wine, or spirits, could loosen the knot in my throat, each drink bringing us still closer, helping us to forget we would soon part.

'Just what do you think you're doing here, Lozerech? Tell me.'

'No one's more surprised than me. Just stick with me and we'll try to work it out.' He was attempting to make light of something which palpably bothered him. But even as he replied, his leg pressed against mine, and we were off, done for, both of us breathing one of those involuntary sighs which punctuate the body's impulses.

They were wonderful and terrible, those days. Wonderful because I find it shamefully easy to live in the moment. Terrible, because I sensed that Gavin was about to offer me his life and that it wasn't an offer he would make twice.

It was only on the last night, in one of those warm little restaurants which cradle you from the harshness of life, that we plucked up the courage to speak. There was no point in even trying in the hotel. Our hands quickly got in the way of any conversation. And the truth was too alarming: we were there in error. We had staged a break-out from our real lives, something for which we'd be punished one day.

While I fiddled with my fish, trying to hide it under the debris on my plate because I knew I couldn't swallow it, Gavin was devouring his food with the concentration he brought to everything he did. And, while he ate, he sketched his vision of the future, as prosaically as he would have negotiated a contract with the Concarneau Fisheries Board. He proposed, at a stroke, breaking off his engagement, changing his job, studying as much as necessary to learn about music and modern art, doing some reading – the classic authors to start with – losing his accent and, finally, marrying me.

He sat there on the other side of the little table, his knees gripping mine, his clear eyes asking if this wasn't a noble sacrifice. They grew troubled as they read in mine that even the offer of his life was not enough.

I should have preferred not to answer at once, not to

murder in two or three words so passionate a love. I wanted to say we could think it over. But his ingenuousness broke my heart. What other man would ever make me so generous and so mad a proposal? Unfortunately Gavin only operated on a straight yes or no. He would rather tear the heart from his breast than put up with the compromise of seeing me but not possessing me.

I was silent for a moment: all I could offer him in return were those frivolous things which are no foundation for life – the crazy desire and the tenderness I felt for him. I didn't want to give up my degree. I didn't want to be a fisherman's wife. I couldn't live in Larmor among his fishermen friends. I didn't want Yvonne for a sister-in-law, or to spend my Sundays at the Lorient stadium, watching him running around in the penalty area. Above all, I didn't want him to sacrifice his job, his accent, any of his strengths and weak-nesses. How did I know I would still love him as an office worker, or even as a shipwright, without the reflection of the sea in his eyes? And would he love himself?

My arguments were useless. His face closed sullenly. He looked dogged, but he couldn't control a quiver at the corner of his mouth. Christ, how I loved that contradiction in him, between the vulnerability and the fierce impulsiveness of his nature. Seeing his pain made me love him even more. I deserved a beating for that.

As we left the restaurant I tried to put my arm round his waist, but he pulled away brusquely.

'If that's how you feel, best I be off tonight. No point in paying the hotel another night,' he said flatly.

For me, giving up even one night was an insult to life, a rejection of the gift we had been offered. But I could not convince him of that. Lozerech was going back to his own kind, filled with bitterness against city girls who fucked up your life, then went off with a clear conscience. He was constructing a version of events which would fit his own world-view.

'You'll be sorry, maybe, that you turned down my offer,' he said. 'Maybe you're too complicated to be happy.'

He didn't look at me. He never looked me in the eye when he criticised me. He reckoned that in a year – well, five at most – he could catch up to my level. He thought you could catch up on anything. He had no idea of the unfair advantages you get from a prosperous upbringing and a privileged education. He thought one got places simply by hard work. And he wasn't one to shirk hard work. What was the point of being brave and industrious if you couldn't conquer obstacles like those? He wouldn't have believed me if I had told him that it isn't just books and hard work which make the difference. It would have seemed too cruel, too unjust.

So I chose lesser arguments, more petty, more acceptable, which reassured him in a way. But the one who reasons is the one who loves less. Gavin already knew this.

The last train for Quimperlé had gone. What joy! Now he would have to come and lie beside me one more time, this brute, who was getting more hostile by the minute. Back at the hotel he asked for another room, but they were all taken. I tried not to let my satisfaction show. As soon as we got to our room he started flinging things into his suitcase, the way they do in films. Then he undressed in silence, hiding his sex to punish me. In bed, I had once more that warm wheat smell of him, but he turned his back on me, that white back of a seaman who has neither the time nor the desire to sun-bathe. His brown neck looked quite different, like a game of Heads, Bodies and Legs. I brushed my lips where the brown and white met below childlike wisps of hair, but he didn't stir. An icy force field of rejection emanated from him, paralysing me, and I lay there, sleepless, as close as I could get without touching him.

In the small hours, sensing that he had dropped his guard, I couldn't stop myself pressing my belly to his back and laying my cheek on his shoulder. In that silent half-sleep, I felt our deepest beings embrace, refusing separation. Outside our will, or, rather, beneath it, our sexes were signalling one to the other. Gavin tried to ignore the message, but it was too powerful for him. He turned suddenly and threw himself on to me without any preliminaries, thrusting into the place that was calling him. He came immediately, hoping to humiliate me, but his mouth stayed glued to mine, and we fell asleep breathing each other in until the cruel break of dawn.

At Montparnasse, under the livid light which seems to be the bane of railway stations, we just couldn't kiss. All he did, as he climbed into the carriage, was put his temple against my cheek, like that first time in the car. Then he turned away immediately to hide his orphaned face, and I made for the exit, my heart full of tears, my mind full of logic, as if they belonged to two different people.

No one spared me a glance. Bereft of the raving desire which I had inspired a few short hours before, I wandered in an indifferent world. Trembling with loneliness I cursed not being able to live our lives according to our desires – my not being able to for sure, and Gavin probably, once he recognised the implications. I knew I was still imprisoned by the prejudices I'd been taught since childhood. And this rigidity of mine, which in those days substituted for character in me, was appalled by his lack of culture, the way he swore all the time, his mottled windcheaters and plaited sandals worn with socks, his sniggering at abstract art. Only the day before he had annihilated an abstract painting with a few annoyingly sensible words. Nor could I forgive him his favourite singers – Rina Ketty, Tino Rossi, Maurice Chevalier – whom I despised, and had annihilated with a few curt words myself. Nor the way he sliced bread towards himself, and cut up the steak on his plate into pieces. Nor the poverty of his vocabulary which cast doubts on the quality of his mind. It was all too much to remedy. And how would he have taken it? Culture inspired a vague mistrust in him. Fancy words were what 'sodding politicos' used to fool ordinary people, 'the lot of them'. Nothing could persuade him that not all politicians were corrupt smooth-talkers – except for the Communists perhaps, for whom he voted automatically, less from conviction than professional solidarity. Aboard their boats trawlermen form a kind of commune, sharing the proceeds of every catch. Gavin took pride in not being a wage slave. Where he came from, what counted was doing one's work well, being honest and having guts. Good health was important and feeling tired a weakness, not far removed from skiving. The value of work lay in its usefulness, not in the time or effort it took.

For Parisians like us who flirted with the avant garde (my father published a modern art magazine), honesty was a rather ludicrous virtue, except in a cleaning lady. Idleness was cheerfully tolerated, so long as it was allied with wit and style. While we despised the village drunk, we felt a certain fondness for the society alcoholics. It might have been amusing to parade my fisherman at a party – after all, my parents were mad about sea shanties and those plaited leather belts with anchor-buckles made by sailors. They admired the

Breton berets and clothes in the traditional red or blue sail-cloth, carefully faded to look authentic, which only summer visitors still wore. They used the Breton farewell, *Kenavo*, when they left the village shop, and were charmed by the Breton name of the village baker, 'Corentin'. My father even wore the local wooden clogs for ten minutes a year, and the spotted socks that went with them. 'Nothing more practical for gardening,' he would proclaim, almost prepared to stuff in the traditional handful of straw – 'so much healthier'.

However, real live fishermen, all hairy and brawny, any-where but on a tuna boat or trawler, noble though they be in their yellow oilskins and thigh boots – ugh! 'I really take my hat off to those men,' but on the oriental rugs of a Paris apartment, with their dirty fingernails and mottled wind-cheaters – ugh! In 1950 class barriers were impenetrable, and I knew I didn't have the strength of character to acclimatise Gavin to these surroundings, immerse him in my culture. And I didn't want to transplant myself into his. He had no idea of how cruel my family could be to someone like him, what he would suffer if we were to get married, nor did he realise how intellectually isolated I would feel with him.

'Why do you have to be so complicated?' he had demanded the night before, making no secret of his hostility. 'Why can't you take things as they come?' Well, I did have to be complicated, actually.

He had promised to telephone before he rejoined his boat, and the thought of that, bleak though it was, made separation less brutal. But the telephone flummoxed him. I should have thought of that. Theirs had been installed only recently, in the draughty front hall of the farmhouse where everyone could hear. For him it was a diabolical contraption, good only for cancelling appointments or announcing deaths. He spoke loudly, articulating each word clearly as if I were deaf. He didn't use my name once. It had been bad enough asking the operator for Paris, knowing she would be wondering what business young Lozerech had there.

'You haven't changed your mind then?' he asked at once.

'It's not a question of changing my mind, Gavin. It's . . . well, I just don't see what else I could do. I wish you'd understand . . .'

'Oh, me! I can't understand anything.'

Silence. Then I asked, 'You're off tomorrow still?'

'That's how you wanted it, isn't it?'

He was right. It was impossible to communicate through this horrible instrument. I felt incapable of saying 'I love you' into it. Terrified he would hang up, I blurted the first thing that came into my head.

'Write to me, won't you? And tell me where I can write back.'

'It's a bit tricky. I'll be living with Marie-Josée's family while I study for my diploma. But I'll send you a card as soon as I get to Concarneau.'

'Oh sure. With your best wishes, I hope.'

Wounded silence. He wasn't one to shout 'bloody hell' down the telephone.

'Right then. I must be off now,' he said with finality, and hung up. The black receiver went back on the wooden wall of the farmhouse.

4
The Next Ten Years

For the next ten years I was far too busy getting on with my life to indulge in nostalgia for my first love. That comes later, when the second love, the one you stake your life on, starts foundering. That's when lost opportunities get irresistibly attractive. Meanwhile, I was moving imperceptibly from girlhood to womanhood, approaching that threshold of thirty when there are several different routes to choose. And whichever I chose I would find myself wondering if this was the final, fixed path, if something of real importance could still happen to me.

People who've turned sixty smile at the callowness of the young. They shouldn't. It wasn't until I had passed the thirty mark that I lost that most priceless of youth's attributes, lightheartedness. Until then I lived my life as though I were immortal. It would have appalled me if I had realised how precarious life is, how my body, instead of being my servant, would become a tyrannical master. Until I was thirty, everything I experienced, even grief, had the charm of novelty.

It was during that lighthearted decade, my twenties, that I got my classics degree followed by a doctorate in History, became an assistant lecturer at the Sorbonne, married Jean-Christophe, a chief cameraman for what was then Gaumont News, and gave birth to a little boy, very blond and freckled, whom we named Loïc Erwann. In the same year, 1952, Gavin married Marie-Josée and before they knew where they were they had produced four children. After our parting he had steered his life back on its original course. Not for him the luxury of brooding. I learned all his news from his

53

mother. He had 'made skipper' she told me, and was fishing off southern Ireland. 'But he says it's a hard life,' she would add and in her eyes I could glimpse the grief she never spoke: two years earlier her youngest son, Robert, then only fourteen, had been swept overboard by a freak wave at night. His body had never been found. Since then she had been more tolerant when her sons admitted to finding the life hard.

Every summer, braving family disapproval, Gavin came back for the annual tuna hunt off the Gascon coast. It was more like a hunt than an ordinary fishing expedition, and he revelled in it; it was the high point of his year. 'Tourist sport', his mother always called it dismissively. It's true that in the Fifties tuna were scarce round there. 'Your brother's doing very well for himself in Mauretania with the crayfish,' she would add slyly, when he visited the farm with Marie-Josée and the children.

Her daughter-in-law was quick to take the cue. 'You can say that again. The sea's crawling with them.' A covetous gleam lit her eye. 'There's the children to think of. And the payments on the house . . .'

At thirty-three, Marie-Josée was firmly enrolled in the ranks of housewives. She was one of those women reduced to being mere mammals who talk about 'the kids' and are 'on the go' from sunrise to sunset, scrubbing the house, digging the vegetables, labouring over the washing. It was only for Mass on Sundays that she took off the flowered overall, pulled out of shape by the homogeneous mass of her bosom. Having lost two teeth and aged ten years during her last pregnancy, she looked middle-aged before her time, more like her mother-in-law than the fleetingly youthful girl Gavin had married a few years earlier.

I passed him sometimes in the village, where he came to

play *boules* on the Sundays he was ashore. His wife's pregnancies hadn't altered *his* looks. He was still the most devastating man in Raguenès. For that matter, in Nevez, Trégunc, Trévignon, Concarneau itself. I should have loved to ruffle his apparent serenity, to find out if he ever thought about me. But he was never alone, so he never had to refer to the wild detour we had once made from our destined paths.

In my early twenties I was sure it would be the richest and most important decade of my life. By their end I was shattered to discover that I had to start again from scratch, stunned that of the ten 'most beautiful years of one's life', I had spent five in profound unhappiness. It was far too long: and for some time I was furious that I'd let myself stagnate so dismally. But you've got to know unhappiness some time, and if it comes in your twenties the damage isn't irreparable, I guess. Afflicted with low self-esteem and a stiff upper lip, I tried to make the most of things, and it was years before I admitted to myself that my marriage was unbearable, indeed damaging to me. The one thing I got from it was the feeling that I had drained my allotted portion of suffering to the dregs.

Naturally I sometimes wondered whether I should have been happier with Gavin. Easy temptation! Playing around with thoughts of what might have been consoles so many married women who, if they were single again, would make exactly the same choice. Anyway, heartbreak is one thing, divorce quite another. They have to be dealt with separately. Life's complicated enough already.

Then one day I woke up to the fact that for five years I hadn't looked at a single man, apart, that is, from the one who was making me so unhappy. This is a state which, though commonplace enough, never seems to prevent its victims, women usually, from persisting in it. That day my deliverance came like lightning, and my convalescence was heavenly. Those nights spent weeping, those days of uncertainty, of self-abnegation, seemed now the more futile in that I failed to win back the man I had loved too well, the man whose vague dissatisfactions and then blatant bad temper I had tried in vain to understand.

The light dawned when my misery was incarnated in the form of a woman director with whom, for several years, he had gone on location. My relief was so intense that the trusting, humble creature I had become very soon seemed a complete stranger. A fool. For a while I still went on hating myself, still mounted various stratagems to win Jean-Christophe back, or at least free myself sooner. But I no longer recognised in myself the blind, paralysed wife I had become. Perhaps you have to spend some time being someone you aren't in order to become the person you really are. Or perhaps there are lots of people within you, and you need to get rid of one before you can try another. At all events, I simply shed the humble, sorrowful George like dead skin. I had played that role for all it was worth, gone through all the prescribed scenes, spoken every line right up to the dénouement, so predictable and tawdry it could have come from any B-movie. Then I discovered a new bent for happiness, an unexpected capacity for laughter and lightheartedness. It isn't just that you're unhappy; it's that you're deprived of the minimum requirement of cheerfulness, the consolation of laughter or, better still, the therapeutic fit of giggles, which leaves you gasping, your sides aching and all tension released. Unhappiness is no joke.

My first symbolic gesture of freedom was to buy myself a bicycle. It wasn't until then I realised how much I had sacrificed for my marriage. There had been that post in a lycée at Abidjan: Jean-Christophe couldn't live anywhere but Paris. There had been my co-ownership of a sailing dinghy at Concarneau: Jean-Christophe got seasick. There were the tours I could have joined, to Athens, Moscow, Mexico: Jean-Christophe hated travelling, especially in groups, especially on those educational tours that were more like scout camp than Club Med. There were the bicycling holidays I enjoyed so much: my husband hated bicycling. His passions were motor bikes, gliding and bridge, all of which I found deadly.

My second gesture was to fold up the bridge table and dump it in the cellar. My Sundays were my own again. No more afternoons when no one would speak to me except to criticise my bids. No more afternoons when even my wittiest friends confined themselves to basic phrases. I couldn't take bridge seriously, yet you're not supposed to joke about it. If I dared I incurred marital wrath and the evening would be poisoned by Jean-Christophe commenting on the afternoon's moves, working out what our score would have been if only I had bid hearts. Well, I bid my heart all right in the end and we divorced without too much damage. I got custody of Loïc 'in view of his tender years', a convenient formula for men since they thought it catastrophic to be lumbered with a young child in those days, and this way they didn't get their egos deflated.

I didn't tell Gavin about the divorce. He'd learn anyway from village gossip. We had always sent one another cards addressed to the whole family. Sometimes I would slip in some ambiguous phrase, which probably didn't mean anything but keeping a little spark of memory alive. Anyway, just then, love was not my main preoccupation.

It wasn't long before Jean-Christophe married again. And

not the lady who had been the cause of my tears. It often happens that when a marriage founders, the person who's provoked it founders too. This filled me with unworthy glee. I had had enough of being worthy. What I longed for was to lead my own life in a new country. So when I was offered a post teaching History and Comparative Literature at Wellesley I jumped at it, and went off to Massachusetts with my eight-year-old son. It was the kind of American campus I'd dreamed of as a student in the gloomy amphitheatres of the Sorbonne, where I dutifully attended lectures before dutifully taking the bus home to my parents every evening.

This heartland of an America which was at peace as the Sixties dawned, this world of teachers and students, was a sheltered haven in which I settled with delight. My life was financially secure, exciting even, and having Loïc with me gave me a little bit of France, made me feel less exiled. The spontaneity and sheer niceness of Americans, their cheerful (and occasionally tactless) intimacy, whatever their position in the university, brought such warmth to my life that I almost forgot the horrors of my marriage, felt almost secure enough to contemplate marrying again. Almost, I said. It took a year with Sidney, a professor in Modern Literature, to alert me to the tender trap I nearly fell into. I was, I realised, too tractable, too fearful perhaps, to stand up to a man I loved. I knew well my tendency to conform, to fit in with another person's way of life. It was a conditioned reflex from my upbringing that I'd never quite rid myself of. This behaviour came so naturally to me that I wasn't aware of the danger until I suddenly woke up to the fact that my share of life had shrunk, my liberty was curtailed, and that I was on the point of being as disenfranchised as I had been with Jean-Christophe. Men, even American men, were still too steeped in privilege – another conditioned reflex alive and kicking – not to install themselves in the roles of the great white hunter or the comfortable pasha.

After one year with Sidney my right to speak had been whittled to half and I no longer carried any weight. In company I always let him steer the conversation. More and more frequently he would interrupt me to make his own point, and less and less did I have the last word. If we started speaking at the same moment I gave way gracefully. And the more sparkling he was, the duller I grew, without realising why. I would ask his permission to go out, even for a professional dinner, and put down my pen or closed my book as soon as I heard his key in the door. I found myself washing his socks or picking up the Y-fronts he'd chucked in a corner of the bedroom. I never saw him rinsing through my stockings or hanging up my coat . . .

At first my relapse manifested itself only in tenuous symptoms, which could only have been recognised by someone who had already suffered the disease. 'That's what we were saying only the other day, weren't we, George?' The 'we' was Sidney *solus*. 'We had a wonderful week in Maine, didn't we, darling?' Darling nodded yes, but was it darling who described it all with such flashes of wit? No. It was Sidney. He fondly included me in our life, more from natural warmheartedness and generosity than from reverence or at least that respect of which every conjugal cocktail needs a few drops. If we had married it wouldn't have been long before it was 'my wife' this, 'my wife' that, 'my wife's a wonderful cook', every utterance of that word 'wife' eroding a bit more of George.

And my name still plagued me in the States, even though George Sand was then all the rage with intellectuals. Her letters to the great men of the day were studied at a number of universities and one of my friends was translating *Consuelo*, which no one read in France at all. As Women's Studies published articles on her, Sand's freedom in love was as much admired as her literary career. It was at Wellesley that I discovered she had written her first novel when she was only fifteen, that *Indiana* had been a huge success, that for nine years she had provided the surroundings in which Chopin had done his best work. And, above all, that she was small with tiny feet! This put paid to the image of her as a devourer of men, a sort of gendarme with black ringlets who, after leading a life of depravity, had redeemed herself with some pious rustic novels. Which is how she was presented in France.

And, even in America, the name still carried overtones of the depraved woman. 'Oh, so your girlfriend's called George as in George Sand,' some of Sidney's colleagues would say significantly, as if I had deliberately chosen the name to collect hordes of lovers – preferably temperamental geniuses younger than myself – and neglect my domestic duties. It was what they expected of a Frenchwoman. Like a fool, I let myself be influenced by their assumptions, and made it a point of honour to prove that I could be an intellectual at the same time as a mother and housewife, and lead an emotional life too. As it happened I was healthy and strong enough to gaily juggle all these roles. Loïc gave every impression of being happy, and Sidney moved about my life quite tactfully. Finding his back to the wall I was building in self-defence, he showed that he loved me enough to let me live on my own but not so much, thank god, as to let resentment or bitterness poison the relationship.

Sidney was a dilettante of love, an epicurean, an artist, one of those men who are able to inspire unconditional love in women without even seeming to try. His looks helped. He was like Leslie Howard, fair hair streaked with grey and hazel eyes behind wire-rimmed glasses. There was a touching air of the ageing student about him, ageing for a student, that is, but young for a man of forty-five. Luckily this easy-going seducer came into my life at a time when I felt equal to the challenge, when, though still cautious, I no longer allowed myself to be put down or to fawn around him like a spaniel – which he would have accepted as his due, without seeming to take advantage, and with his customary casual elegance.

I went back to France every summer, sometimes with Sidney, so that Loïc could see his father and, more important, get to know his native country. And every other year I spent Christmas with Frédérique and her husband and children at a holiday club in some tropical location. The winter we went to Casamance I was thirty-three, a wonderful age. My eyes were very blue under dark eyebrows, I still had the figure of a girl and my time in the States had given me a relaxed, almost insolent confidence in manner and in the way I dressed. Now Frédérique and I were in Dakar together. We were planning a day's shopping, an activity which usually sends husbands bolting for cover. Antoine, my brother-in-law, had gladly agreed to look after the children for us, so there we were, Frédérique and I, crouching in front of a stall in the market, being tempted once again by native kaftans. Their colours are incredibly strong, magnificent in the trop-ical sun. All the same we knew that we'd throw them away in the end, as usual, having experimented with them as table-cloths, napkins, bedspreads, curtains or even, rashly, as hostess gowns, until those treacherous, hanging sleeves had swept enough fine china off surfaces in the restricted space of our city apartments. I knew all this, but was still on the verge of buying something in vivid red and yellow – colours which I loathe at home – when I heard my name. I was crouching, knee-high to whoever was addressing me, but even without looking up I knew at once who it was. There were the eyes I remembered from Raguenès, the mouth I knew from the hotel near Montparnasse, those prizefighter's shoulders, the stance so familiar, legs a little apart, feet firmly planted. There was everything I had managed to forget and never rediscovered in our brief encounters in Brittany. We were miles from home, yet, suddenly, we had come home to each other.

'George,' he said again, tenderly, looking at me in a way that he had not allowed himself since . . . Oh god, how long was it?

He took both my hands to pull me up. It was as if we were in a bubble, silenced, moved, oblivious to Frédérique who was out there somewhere, uttering sounds which seemed to come from a great distance. Eventually she managed to drag us off to a nearby café, where the tinkle of ice in our glasses of pastis brought us back to earth. We began by exchanging news from home, and then the basic details of our respective lives. These were so alien as to become incommunicable. It wasn't long before we were reduced to gazing at our glasses, shaking our heads, and wondering desperately how to break the silence. At this point Frédérique took the initiative which was to change the course of our lives.

'I've got to leave you for a bit. There's something I must buy. I promised my daughter I'd get her one of those ivory bracelets, and someone's told me about a shop where there are some lovely ones. Let's meet at the bus, George, say in half an hour?'

'I must be off too,' Gavin said tentatively.

Logic dictated a reply like 'Well, goodbye then. See you some time.' A phrase appropriate to our situation, after all. Then Lozerech would have shaken my hand, gone off, and never become my Gavin. It needed only a word from him. But he'd never find it. And if he'd found it he'd never have said it.

'Oh, come on! After all these years it's silly to say goodbye the minute we've met again. Why don't we have dinner together? Just we two, I mean.'

Gavin looked awkward. 'The thing is . . . my wife's here with me.'

'Marie-Josée here? In Dakar?' My vision of a nostalgic *tête-à-tête* evaporated. I should have loved to have had a sentimental dinner with this antithesis of Sidney. I probably wouldn't have found a thing to say except that I was still insanely attracted by his body. That's always a good start, anyway . . .

He explained that his ship was in dry dock after something had gone wrong with the engines. They were going to have to wait for a spare part, so he had taken the chance to ask Marie-Josée to join him because he only saw her for three months a year. I didn't say anything. Gavin didn't suggest anything. Well, what else did I expect? Practical men like him don't burden themselves with memories from thirteen years ago.

'Well then, the three of us could have dinner,' I persisted.

He shuddered, knitted his bushy eyebrows, bleached to auburn by the African sun, as if what he was about to say was costing him an immense effort.

'I don't want to be with you as if we were strangers.'

'So you'd rather not be with me at all?'

'You could put it like that,' he said drily.

Silence. The sun was setting quickly, making the moment so brief, so vibrant with the presentiment that men have always felt at close of day, of some miracle. He spoke again.

'It was tough, you know, getting back to normal after that last time. I don't like not being in charge of my life. I'm not an acrobat, me.'

He meant it, I saw, and a surge of tenderness prevented me from teasing him further. He liked to think of himself as rock hard, but I knew how passionate he really was, and how vulnerable. There was nothing to be gained by raking over old memories. I could just picture us in some hotel room, trying to recapture the magic of our youth; me, trying out some of the techniques I'd learned with Sidney in the hope of enslaving this stubborn creature. No doubt he had resigned himself to unimaginative sex with his wife for a few weeks each year, and to the whores of Abidjan or Pointe Noire for the rest of the time, while his true passion went into his work. He hadn't even asked what it was I did at Wellesley. He spoke only of his own projects. The first nylon seine-nets had just made their appearance on the huge, six-hundred-horsepower Californian fishing boats, which would put the old tuna-boats of Brittany and the Vendée out of business if they insisted on hanging on to their traditional ways. 'Those nets can be more than a kilometre long, can you credit it? Forty acres they cover. They'll clean up here too before long. And we're still using live bait. No wonder we bring back less fish. It's done for, our kind of fishing.'

'So then what will you do?'

'Just have to do like the other buggers, won't we?'

He regarded 'the other buggers' – Basques, Spaniards, Yanks – with ferocious resentment. He wanted the sea to himself. Every skipper is a buccaneer at heart, Lozerech more than most. Anything that sailed the Atlantic was an enemy boat, unless it came from Concarneau. Except for the men of Nevez, Trégunc or Trévignon, anyone who dared trawl, harpoon or seine-net so much as one fish was at best a good-for-nothing, at worst a robber and in any case a looter and a shit. I listened as he talked of his life, with unassuming courage and total lack of humour, both perhaps the result of being at sea too long. There were one or two grey hairs at his temples, paradoxically emphasising the youthful curl of his lips. Deep-sea fishermen never really grow up, living as they do in that small, closed society. It's always the same crew, labouring at the same tasks, laughing at the same jokes, sharing the same profits or losses from the same work. Exiled, far from their families, always looking forward to the end of their spell away, they are imprisoned in a kind of collective childhood. They don't belong to the real world, where people read newspapers every day, vote, go for a drink, take a walk on Sundays. So over the years Gavin had changed a lot less than I had.

The brief tropical twilight came down like a curtain. Only Gavin's eyes glimmered in his sun-browned face with a trace of light from the sky. On summer nights in Brittany, too, after night has fallen and the lighthouses are sending their beams along the coast, the sea still holds a pale glimmer, what my father called 'residual light'. It was a bit of residual love, perhaps, which prompted my impulsive question.

'Lozerech, do you propose to talk about nothing but fishing for the rest of your life? Isn't there anything else you want to know about? Isn't there any room in your life for some craziness? All right, you don't like that word. Let's say, escape . . . something different at least?'

He was taken aback, but began to give it serious thought. I persisted. 'I don't mean changing your life completely. I just mean taking a bit of time to spoil yourself, give yourself a present – do something spontaneous . . .'

'You don't go giving yourself presents much, not in my line of work, you don't. Maybe I'm wrong, but that's the way it is.'

He gazed into the distance, his great hands lying heavily in front of him on the table. They looked like the big crabs the Bretons call 'sleepers'.

'That's the way it is,' he said again. There might have been a shade of nostalgia in his tone but I always want to puke when people say 'That's the way it is.'

'What do you mean, that's the way it is? It's only you who thinks it has to be like that! You've given up, that's what. There's no such thing as fate. People just say there is with hindsight.'

Gavin's face closed up. He hated it when you called his simple tenets into question.

'Before we have to go,' I continued with a smile, 'before we get cross with each other, tell me something. I've been wanting to ask you for years, and now it's been so long you can tell me. What do you really think about our meeting? Was it a failure? Or is it something that still matters to you?'

'A bit of both,' Gavin admitted. 'Time was, I'd rather never have known you. But that's over. Now, whenever I get back to Raguenès I ask after you, you know. But there was no way of getting in touch. I wouldn't have dared, and besides . . . Anyway, I wouldn't have known what to say.'

We were finishing our second pastis. Gavin never drank

gin or whisky, and I didn't want to underline our differences by ordering a 'Parisienne's' drink.

'Well, I might as well tell you that I couldn't forget you either. It's as if I had lost something important in life after I lost you. It wasn't something I'd ever found, just glimpsed. Funny, isn't it?'

'"Today you are tender as the first woman,"' Gavin recited. '"But the nights are as cold as night." There you are, you see. I remember your poem. I learned it by heart.'

I put my hand on his arm, which, with its reddish, curling fleece, never looked quite naked. Did his skin still smell of wheat, I wondered.

'I'd give . . . I don't know what, to take you in my arms here, right now,' he said, his voice choked with emotion. Everything had been going so smoothly until that moment, but those words went like a bolt of lightning straight between my legs and then right into my heart. We had just entered a zone of turbulence. My eyes dropped from his to his mouth which always betrayed his confusion. But Gavin was steadfast. He still imagined that he'd get clear of this moment.

'Well, time to be off,' he said, looking at his watch. Like most seamen, he wore it on the inside of his wrist. I exploded.

'That's the third time you've said that! Whenever we have to part you're *off*. What does *off* mean? Giving up? Back to the old routine?'

'Fuck it! What else can I do?' he shouted.

'I don't know. What about going off the rails? We're not a couple of lambs, going meekly off to the slaughter. You're abroad for the better part of the year. Surely we could meet somewhere.'

He stared at me, clearly taken aback by the turn of events.

'You've changed, *Va Karedig*.'

'Probably because I've lived in the States. I can tell you, no one there lets good manners spoil things for them. They go for it. Especially the women. Does that bother you?'

'I don't know about being bothered, but I do know what I want. And to hell with it.'

He stood up, paid for the drinks, drew me away from the neon of the café, then pulled me to him. Or perhaps I threw myself on him, I can't be sure which. In spite of the years that had passed I knew at once the depth of his kiss, knew the chip on his tooth and the sweetness of his tongue on mine, scarcely moving as we infused each other with our poisons.

We moved apart at last, both of us with gratitude in our eyes that we still exercised this immense fragile power over each other, that life still granted us this gift. I broke the spell at last.

'This time we really do have to be off,' I said, to break the spell. 'The bus leaves in ten minutes.'

Frédérique was waiting for me. And Marie-Josée was waiting for her husband down in the port. Our lives were closing in around us once again. But, inadvertently, a little hope had been admitted. Like children who have succeeded in tricking the grown-ups, we found ourselves laughing with pleasure. I watched him leave, loving his easy, rolling walk. A lot of men keep their bodies stiff above their moving legs but every part of Gavin – his feet, his thighs, his hips, even his shoulders – seemed to move in rhythm, like those slow-motion shots of jaguars running.

We hadn't arranged to see each other again in Dakar. The only way I wanted to meet him was unfettered by family ties, somewhere at the back of beyond. But there's nothing more difficult for a deep-sea fisherman than finding a clear week. The fish come first. They must be pursued, caught, frozen, sold. Then there's the boat. And the boat-owners. And any time over belongs to the family. That doesn't leave a lot of room for the unexpected.

It was almost a year before we could get our expedition off the ground. Things weren't helped by the fact that it would never have occurred to Gavin to buy a plane ticket for New York, say, or Kenya, to see anyone who wasn't either ill or dying. Because of his strict moral code, he was already paying a high price in terms of guilt. Money for the family was sacred. His own desires were not.

It could have been anywhere, some dreary harbour per-haps, but luck took us to the Seychelles. Gavin had been posted there by the Concarneau Fisheries Board, who wanted a work survey to see if it was worth basing their boats there. Having a professional alibi meant he could hide from the unpalatable truth that he was taking a week away from that precious family of his to relive something incomprehensible, something he would never have dared to describe as love but which had shaken him to his foundations twice in his life so far. Still more uncomprehensible was that a woman would travel six thousand miles for no reason other than her desire for him. Him! Lozerech! If anyone had ever prophesied this he would have laughed in their face. So from the moment he got to the Seychelles, ten days before I did, he vacillated between guilt and joy, wondering if the whole thing wasn't the delusion of a couple of lunatics or some evil spell cast by Satan.

5
Dem Faraway Seysel I'lan's

Once upon a time, in a remote archipelago in the Indian Ocean, a seafarer and an historian met through a series of extraordinary chances. Or was it through imperious necessity? There was nothing to bring them together except a desire so physical they dared not call it love. So intense was this passion that it left them both incredulous, mistrustful, sure that each dawn would bring them to their senses. Both were in a state of wonder, as you or I would have been, at having stumbled into that mysterious realm explored only by the poets, who, even now, have not succeeded in mapping it all.

There is no way I can describe that encounter in the first person. I can only offer George's testimony and try to comprehend all the evidence on desire – perhaps the body's ultimate deception – by hiding behind a pronoun less intimate than 'I'.

So. It was in the little airport of the Seychelles, in the Sixties still a British possession, that a fisherman, tortured by doubt, anxiety and remorse, waited for an academic. Too late for regrets: she was about to come down the steps of the twin-propeller plane from Nairobi, and he would have to open his arms to this stranger, who taught god-knows-what god-knows-where in America. At first glance there was nothing to distinguish him – deeply tanned, in light trousers and, for once, without his seaman's cap – from the British civil servants in khaki shorts and long socks or the businessmen there to forget the burdens of their wealth in the excitement of big-game fishing. But he was one of the few without dark glasses and George picked him out immediately in that little crowd, stockier than the others, though no taller, an eyebrow anxiously raised. He was wearing one of those short-sleeved shirts which very few men can carry off. It strained over those huge biceps, designed to heave a drowning man by the collar from the Roaring Forties. With meticulous care, he had chosen it from a repulsive collection, taking the worst of the lot – a horrendous orange print covered in red palm trees and black women with baskets on their heads. Not a very auspicious start. She waved but he didn't move, hanging back a little from the others. He wasn't one to throw himself at you.

She wasn't exactly overcome with impulsive love either. The journey had been exhausting, and all she could muster was a faint smile, while asking herself what on earth had possessed her to set the whole thing up. The arrangements had been harassing and she had spent thousands of dollars and travelled thousands of miles just to meet someone she had kissed only once in the last twelve years. What sort of casting error had allotted her the role of bed-partner to the son of a Raguenès farmer? Quickly she counted up the positive things: his physique for a start; she had never in her life encountered such a body. Then those powerful wrists. Perfect for a seaman. And for a lover . . . as we all know. And the coppery fleece of hair on his arms. And his fingers, which emerged roughly drawn from his farm-labourer's palms, like a badly finished sculpture. She would just have to make believe she had won a trip to an isle of dreams with 'The Sexiest Man of the Year', chosen from a line-up of famous hunks.

When you've come so far to meet someone, the only thing you can do is fling yourself in his arms. George would never have been so brazen in France or anywhere in Europe, but here, liberated by distance, disorientation and the intense heat, she did. Gavin relaxed a little, though he was uncomfortable masquerading as a rich tourist. And he had always despised errant husbands, yet here he was, errant himself. But these inhibitions vanished, electrified by desire the moment George was in his arms.

In public they could exchange only anodyne words, their awkwardness gradually yielding to a strange exhilaration. George-without-an-s and Lozerech here! Together! It must be some huge joke which only they were party to. Once through customs, they climbed into the convertible jeep which Gavin had rented and drove to the hotel. She found that he had booked two rooms.

'You can't really think I've flown thousands of miles to sleep alone?' she asked tenderly.

'I had an idea you'd not want me around all the time, so's you'd get some rest,' he said, the hypocrite!

'Look, we could hang on to it until tomorrow, see how it goes.'

'It's too late to cancel anyway,' said Gavin, ever practical. 'We'll use the best one tonight, the one I booked for you.'

It was vast, with a big colonial bed draped with mosquito netting, and huge windows opening on the long sandy beach bordered with palm trees which clattered their fronds in the breeze. George, who had never seen the Indian Ocean before, was amazed by the sky, leaden at the horizon, bright blue above, painting the sea with all its changing colours. So unlike Senegal, where a hazy sky merges with the misty blank horizon.

Together, they leaned over the verandah, pretending to be absorbed in the view, but their bodies sneaked closer. The second their arms touched, their veins flooded with the first wave of surrender, which swept away the mountain their separation had made between them. Yet still Gavin didn't dare snatch this woman in his arms, carry her into the bedroom, pin her down. Still the woman didn't dare put her lips to the neck of that frightful shirt, kiss the soft fuzz on his chest, run her hands over the narrow hips which, contrasting with the stocky body, moved her so strangely. They stayed, side by side, listening to the mounting tide in which, together, they were about to drown. Already they were floating, their feet no longer touching bottom.

It was Gavin who finally turned, went back into the airy room and pulled back the bedspread and the top sheet. Before them lay the bed, an undefiled beach, a blank map, waiting for them to draw their own continents and islands. Their mouths never separating, they tore off each other's clothes, ran their hands over each other's ribs, thighs, arms, exploring the hollow of a back, the curve of a buttock with minute attention, revelling in an erotic meandering which, as their deepening tremors told them, was leading to that moment when his sex and hers would come together, never to part.

They fell on the bed, searching the other's body with still greater intimacy. Once again they were taking possession of each other, but as if for the first time, when it seems both indecent and utterly enticing. George smiled as her hand found his balls once more. They were so compact, so tight to his groin, she would have known them among a thousand others. Well, seven or eight. She played with them for a bit out of politeness, but it was the next part which really interested her. She might have had slightly ambivalent feelings about the texture of his scrotum, but his penis felt completely right, just as it should be. As she caressed it she was astonished anew by the way it felt – not hard like wood, not even like cork, say, but hard and soft at the same time, like nothing else in the world but another penis in a similar state of arousal.

Using only her thumb and forefinger, she explored it from top to bottom, tapping it gently, smiling to herself each time it curvetted like an eager horse. It was silky smooth, like a coconut tree, curved in the same curious way, and the colour of ivory, not purple at all. The word 'tumescent' wasn't right for it. Freed now from the foreskin, the rounded tip reminded George of the walking stick an old soldier had carved for her while he was convalescing at the Concarneau hospital in 1944. The knob had been in the shape of those First World War helmets with a curving brim. Now she squeezed Gavin's knob in her hand and indulged herself momentarily in the dread of its imminent intrusion. It was too big for her, that much was plain.

'You don't by any chance have the same model in a smaller size?' she whispered in his ear. 'This one will never fit.'

His only response was to swell still further in her hand, the bastard. She was revelling both in her fear and in Gavin's increasing urgency, torn between his desire to continue caressing her and his volcanic need to explode in her. Immediately.

With heroic, loving self-control he began his approach, circling all five fingers round what became suddenly the centre of the universe for both of them, a great sea waiting to engulf them, drown them. She held herself motionless, so as not to miss the last tremor of the maelstrom mounting in her. His fingers reached the edge of the cavity, but the moment he touched those glistening lips he could not stop himself from plunging in. Crudely, with no refinements, unable to dictate his own rhythm, he was rushed towards climax by the beast awakened within, which insisted on leading the dance. Both lost themselves in that limbo where passion is submerged by pleasure, which in its turn rekindles passion, where there's no way of separating one from the other, the start from the finish.

'Sorry, I'm going too quick. Sorry!' he kept saying, and she kept murmuring that sometimes she liked him to be a brute, though he couldn't believe it and that was why she loved him. He wasn't the kind of man who imagined that women enjoy a bit of rough treatment.

'I couldn't wait to be inside you again,' he muttered. 'Even if it meant hurting you. Forgive me.'

'No, no, you make me feel so good. George's arms tightened round him.

At last he nested in her like the Beloved of the Song of Songs, deceptively still and gloriously weighty. She loved his weight, she loved this artificial lull. Before long he sought her mouth again, cutting off speech, switching on their bodies. She felt his penis start to swell again, as if it were being inflated by a bicycle pump. In little bursts at first, then more and more strongly, the shameless lodger installed itself, expanding to occupy all the available space, pushing out the sides, extending to the furthest tip.

'Feel free,' she whispered. 'Make yourself at home.'

His answer was a rhythmic groan, and she murmured over and over again how much she loved him, how it moved her so deeply that he couldn't wait sometimes, how she wasn't going to worry about her own orgasm now, she could wait, she didn't want to ruin it, she adored just missing it, just anticipating, storing it up. She knew she had nothing to worry about with Gavin; he was sure to flush it out sooner or later, wherever it was lurking. Besides she enjoyed this latency, this expectation which was to be with them all their waking hours, wherever they went, at meals, out walking, on the beach, in the sun. This perpetual love, this passion which refused to die down, keeping a permanent vibration between them, a vital pulsation which made each moment they spent together precious beyond measure.

An orgasm is a solitary affair, in the end. As it approaches, you find yourself concentrating on the fine mechanics of pleasure, and, at the peak, it is in yourself alone that the tension breaks. But tonight George didn't want to be alone for a single second. She wanted pleasure which seeks no resolution, which meanders so as to last, carrying both partners on the same breaker, blinding them with the certainty that there is nothing to touch times like these, when you use all your senses to the utmost to arrive at that hinterland which is everyone's lost domain.

For the first time since they had known each other Gavin and George had a future ahead. Ten days! Ten whole days which made them feel rich, idle, unhurried. And they hadn't even unpacked. They staggered out of bed. For the first time they would be hanging their clothes in the same wardrobe. As they went back and forth, they looked at each other with a tender gratitude, for what they had received, for what they gave. Gavin had brought almost no clothes with him: his case was taken up with a trammel-net. Incredible! Only a fisherman or a madman would think of taking a trammel-net on holiday. His excuse was that he had promised to bring it for Conan, a Breton friend of his here – he had Breton friends in every port – who was lending them his boat. They would all three go fishing, it was already planned.

'Haven't you got any other shirts?' demanded George, dangling the poisonously red article from two fingers.

'Why? Don't you like it? I got it in Dakar.'

'It'd be fine in Dakar. I wouldn't have to see it there. But here, I'm afraid, I'll have to confiscate it. It's making me cross-eyed.'

'Whatever you like, *Karedig*. It's great having you look after me. No one's ever told me what to buy or what to wear, and I don't know a thing about it. Anyway, I don't give a damn. I just buy what's there.'

He stood before her in all his glory – sleek, strong, his eyes bluer than ever beneath their brown lashes – just forty, on the borderline between youth and maturity.

'*I* give a damn, I assure you. I like you to look as good in clothes as you do without clothes. What's more, if you don't mind, I'm going to get rid of those god-awful sandals while we're about it. You've got sneakers or your own bare feet.'

'What about my trousers? Are you going to steal those too?'

'Oh, I might let you wear those. From time to time.'

He hugged her tightly against that indecent sex of his, moved that George was being more maternal than his mother had ever been.

On their second day they wandered around Victoria, the archipelago's miniature capital city on the main island, Mahé. Although the British had seized it after the Napoleonic wars, it was still redolent of the French culture they had failed to eradicate. Now that the Seychellois were to be granted their independence, the new postage stamps were printed with the French-Creole phrase '*Zil elwagnées Sesel*' – 'dem faraway Seysel i'lan's'. The France of Louis XIV had left indelible marks here! The names of the islands could have come from any Rameau opera, while the names of the caves – Poules-Bleues, A-la-Mouche, Bois de Rose, Boudin – or of the islands – Aride, Félicité, Curieuse, Cousin, Cousine, Praslin – had clearly been dreamed up by legendary buccaneers and navigators. Queen Victoria made her presence felt in only one place, but it was in the very heart of Mahé de la Bourdonnais, which wasn't about to forgive her.

Wherever they went, Gavin and George were accompanied by a tropical downpour. Only when they set out to explore the neighbouring beaches in the jeep did they discover that less than fifteen miles away a burning sun had shone all day. Because it is set among mountains Mahé is always rainy, so they decided to make the most of the boat offered by Conan and go to the island of Praslin, sheltered by its coral reef, and only two hours' sail from Victoria.

They had never sailed together before, and Gavin was delighted to do the honours of his element for George. She was seeing him at his most attractive – quick, competent, sparing of his movements, as a seafarer should be. His was a longstanding relationship with the sea, so he was wise to all its tricks. Except, perhaps, for the final trick, which might yet leave him sleeping down below.

They were lashed by three brief storms and laughed together at the tropical warmth and violence of it all. George couldn't remember laughing like that for years, laughing simply for the pleasure of it, laughing with joy at feeling like a child again. Perhaps you can surrender yourself so wholly to laughter only when you're with someone you've surrendered to wholly in passion. Could George imagine Gavin laughing like that with his wife? Where he came from it would more likely be guffawing with the other men on nights out. The women laughed guiltily before turning back to their work: 'That's enough of that. Better get on with it now.' In a hard life like theirs there was bound to be a distance between man and wife after the first few years. How could they discuss their work with each other – he at sea, she in the house? The toil of farm or factory is a long way from the easy laughter of childhood.

They came on Praslin from the east, and, after constantly changing their minds, set the trammel-net in Volbert Cove, on the edge of what they thought was a sandbank and some shallows, in a promising-looking place. Conan often fished there, though using a drag-net rather than a trammel.

They berthed at Fisherman's Village, where Conan had lent them his dilapidated palm-fringed bungalow on the tiny island of Chauve-Souris, a few cable-lengths from the main island, and set in water of the first diamond. (Well, why not? You have diamonds of the first water.) Nobody could have stayed there long unless in the first stages of passionate love. There was no other way of filling those endless afternoons, the hours of ceaseless rain, the long evenings when you're hemmed in by the jungle and deafened by the cacophony of shrieking birds, batrachians and other horrors.

At sunrise next day they borrowed a canoe to reclaim their net from a young local, Hippolyte, who surveyed their operations with a sardonic eye. He obviously found it absurd for holidaying Europeans to be playing at what he had to do year round simply to survive. His smile broadened when he saw where the 'tourists' had put their net. True, it held four sharks, a blue-spotted ray, some mullet and a beautiful carangue, but it also contained pounds and pounds of dead coral, bristling with needle points and razor-sharp edges. They would have either to abandon the net – unthinkable for a fisherman – or free it from the seabed, mesh by mesh from the tangle of crumbling, sharp, greyish coral, which meant hours of labour.

As the three of them set about the thankless task from the boat, heads down, backs to the sun, hands scratched and bleeding, a brown creature, about three inches long, detached itself from a thwart and fell on to George's ankle. She screamed.

'Centipede!' yelled Hippolyte, leaping to his feet in fright. As he pursued it along the bottom of the boat with the gaff he watched George from the corner of his eye, evidently expecting her to pass out instantly. Her ankle was swelling visibly, but she felt honour-bound not to make a fuss in front of Gavin.

'Yes, I can feel it,' she replied to the boy's anxious enquiries. 'I'll be all right though.' This was pure bravado.

He concluded that it hadn't been particularly poisonous.

'If it bite you proper, you be howlin',' he reassured them. There was clearly some point on the scale of suffering where a European woman was supposed to start howling. But, as she returned to her task, George realised, not for the first time in her life, that courage in the face of adversity wasn't going to earn her any praise. Both men had forgotten the incident, and were concentrating on the net. Young Hippolyte was no figure from *Uncle Tom's Cabin*, ready to fling himself down and suck the poison from her ankle.

Now he offered Gavin his knife to cut the dense tangle of netting away from the coral, but Gavin wouldn't hear of it. You don't damage a tool of your trade, especially if it belongs to someone else. Hippolyte gave them up for mad white folks. Still, Gavin and George persevered until well into the evening. Their hands were flayed and their fingers criss-crossed with cuts, but Conan would get his net back perfect, or nearly.

The foot, however, was far from perfect. The wait hadn't done it any good and it was swollen and misshapen, the skin stretched shiny and hot, the pain searing. Gavin was angry with himself at not having taken it more seriously at the time. Little did they know that, thanks to the centipede, they were about to quit the blind world of lovers for a kind of connubial closeness.

He settled George in the shade with her leg up and used every single ice-cube in the tiny calor-gas refrigerator on cold compresses. Then he hitched a lift to Praslin and hired a bicycle to search out bandages and surgical spirit. He was up and down all night, bringing her drinks. And all this he did with such solicitous concern that George felt no suffering could ever have been so delightful. In the guide book they read that a centipede sting was the most dreaded of all, but they weren't going to let an insect wreck this precious week. George mustered all her strength to make little of her pain, trying to detach her consciousness from her poisoned foot, mentally isolating it in the hope of stopping the poison spreading.

Her foot, by now almost spherical, was less of a burden in the sea, so, as they were only a step or two from the soothing water they stayed there all day. Gavin massaged the leg, carefully avoiding the discoloured area of the bite, and gradually the swelling subsided. 'Just let me,' he would say, 'I know what I'm doing.' At sea it's the skipper or his second-in-command who has to act as doctor, surgeon even, when there's an accident, a broken bone, an abscess.

Disoriented by not being engaged in love-making, they did what first came into their heads. That is to say, they actually began talking to each other, discovering who the other was, apart from being of the opposite sex. Up to then their only exchanges had been lovers' words. This new way of relating made them a bit shy. George decided it was a good time to familiarise Gavin with her own topography. She wanted him to know what was most important for her, how she spent those huge tracts of time when they were apart, why her work mattered to her as his mattered to him. She also wanted him to learn about the world around them. And where better than here in the Seychelles, whose history could be read in every corner, where successive conquests by France and England, and by pirates too, had left their mark? Gavin had never read a guide book in his life. For him the sea was a work place, like a factory or a farm, or a mine to be exploited. He never gave a thought to the great explorers who had furrowed it before him. The islands were there so he could work from them, and that's all there was to it. Tuna fish had been created to feed mankind, he'd been put on earth to catch them, his children to live by those tuna fish once he had caught them. He didn't have the time to think about the past. Thinking too much was a luxury not for the likes of him. He would never have imagined that it might actually give him pleasure. But stuck here in enforced idleness, and George a history teacher . . . well, he'd give it a go.

To begin with she told him stories of slaughter and pillage, so as not to frighten him off. It's bandits and adventurers that appeal to the boys.

'Have you read about any of the famous explorers?'

'You know how it is. There's not a lot to read on board, just some thrillers and comic books. Hold on, though. I remember reading something about Christopher Columbus. It was a book I got one prizegiving at Quimperlé.'

'I'll get a book on the history of the Seychelles as a present for you. It'll be a souvenir of our time here. Honestly, it's as good as a thriller, with the French and the English taking turns to chase each other off, changing the names of places every time, changing the religion every time, getting rich, slaughtering each other. And in the end it was the pirates who got the loot. Apparently there's stacks of hidden treasure all around these islands. The Seychelles were a pirates' lair when they were desert islands.'

'Pirates,' mused Gavin. 'That must be a lot more fun than being a burglar.'

'You, my darling? You could never be a pirate! You're far too moral, Lozerech my boy. Even being a lover makes you guilty.'

Gavin gave her a tender punch on the leg, taking care to avoid her ankle. He liked to be talked about, he wasn't used to it.

'No, what I see you as is a gallant captain, faithful to his sovereign. Every time you got back from one of your voyages, you'd render up to him scrupulously all the gold and diamonds you'd won from the natives or the enemy – that wouldn't be robbery then. You'd account for every last doubloon. And, as your reward, you'd be thrown into a dungeon for having offended some bigwig with your honesty. Or else you'd be thrown overboard by your crew, mutinying because you wouldn't let them have any of the king's treasure.'

'You think I'm such a bloody fool?'

'You bet I do. In those days your kind of honesty paid even less than it does now. I'll tell you what did pay sometimes, though – being a great lover.'

'There you are. I might have had some luck with that if

I'd been a pirate. At least, if I'm to believe what you say. Of course, I wouldn't know,' he added with false modesty.

They burst into laughter. On matters of sex they felt gloriously equal. George couldn't resist an exploratory caress, just to make sure everything was as it should be, and even concentrating on a history lesson he grew under her hand.

'I'm not kidding. Tahiti yielded to France because Bougainville's men were better lovers than Captain Cook's. Queen Pomare, Tahiti's ruler, found the English parson, Pritchard, such a bad lay that she offered her territory to the French after spending a few nights with some Lozerech in the French expeditionary fleet. I know, I'll give you *Bougainville's Voyages* too. You'll love it.'

'Why don't you give me your own book? I can't get over it, you writing a book. I always thought writers weren't like us ordinary folk. You know, they're untouchable . . .'

'No, I don't know! You seem pretty good at touching writers. Anyway, I don't see you caring for my book much. It's pretty academic. It's all about women and revolutions. Not exactly two of your most favourite subjects. Or let's say you've not given them much thought, so you don't know if it interests you or not.'

'Go ahead. Tell me again what a thickhead I am.'

'That's just what I *am* telling you.' And George feinted playfully towards him, as he had done earlier.

'I sometimes wonder what I'm doing, messing about with someone like you.' Gavin wasn't sure how to take George's teasing.

'And me with you. Think about it. We'll just have to openly admit that we're in love with each other, thickhead that I love.' Clasping him round the neck she drew him down towards her. There was no more thinking or teasing for as long as that kiss lasted.

'You fascinate me, if you really want to know,' resumed George, once they had surfaced. 'I'm crazy about your character. Yes, that dreadful character of yours. I adore your sweetness. And you're so clever at love. Most men haven't got the first idea. But you . . . you're certainly not a thickhead when it comes to love. So you see! As for my book, it's only a thesis. Tell you what, I'll send it to you with a compromising dedication, so you'll have to read it in secret and bury it in the garden.'

The sun was setting behind the bougainvillaea-twined verandah. George reminded herself to tell Gavin that this plant was all that remained of the great Boungainville, not any of his islands. They drank rather too much of the local punch, and George told him all about her life at Wellesley. She talked freely, like most people of her class and background. Gavin and his kind spoke only when they had to. Few confidences could be exchanged, even between best friends on a boozy evening, and those there were would be told jokingly. It wasn't done to discuss one's feelings – as unthinkable as old Granny Lozerech wearing anything but black, or his mother sleeping late in the morning. It was the height of emotion to come out with phrases like 'It was a bit rough then', or 'Things could have been better', punctuated with a thoughtful 'You can say that again and all', followed by a silence in which each man recalled his experiences. But tonight, his tongue loosened by punch, Lozerech temporarily forgot his role as taciturn fisherman. At last he was allowing part of his deepest self to be glimpsed, and, even more astonishingly, by a woman. He wasn't even talking about love. He was speaking, at last, about what was most important to him.

This could have been a kind of violation of what was best in him but he had a dispensation in that George too was tipsy with pills and punch. They hadn't gone out to dinner because of her ankle and Gavin never stopped talking while they feasted on tropical fruits: fishing off Dakar and the Ivory Coast; the way each voyage was a fresh challenge; the thrill when they found a shoal, and the way the sea boiled as the fish came to the surface, wild for the bait, and the powerful bamboo rods you had to grab and the ramp which hid the men from their prey. Frantic, they all got, everyone from the chief engineer to the cook, ready for the spoils. And there was that moment, brutal as making love – yes, that's what he said – when, with one last straining of his every nerve a man brings his tuna on deck, as much as forty pounds of flailing fish. Voracious they are too, those great fish, and the man are excited, blood all over their oilskins, and the landed fish keep thumping on the deck, then you have to get the hooks out and throw the lines back in the water . . .

George had already noticed that Gavin got more and more Breton when he talked about his work. He loved explaining to her the code, the jargon of his trade, loved talking about the way they found the tuna banks, and fished for the sardines with which they baited their hooks, all the preparations for the big confrontation. Yes, he allowed, it was a lot more work than fishing with a seine-net, what with extracting the hooks and rebaiting them over and over and, yes, there could be trouble sometimes, they went so quick that men got swept overboard. But what a great sport! His eyes shone with admiration for his prey, his adversary. 'It's a grand beast, you know, gives you a great fight. You should see it. Thirteen of us once, we brought in three hundred of 'em in under half an hour. Huge ones too.'

'It must be really impressive,' George said.

'Great, yes.' The word 'impressive' didn't figure in his vocabulary.

'But it's all finished now,' he continued with a fisherman's fatalism. 'The owners run everything these days. They change the boats, the crews, just how they want. We don't have any say in it. Line-fishing, that's over. Those Yanks, with the nets they use, they can get ten tons of tuna a day. We're lucky if we can get ten tons a trip.' He had an absent expression. 'Aye. Our way's done for.' Suddenly he was very far away from George.

'But you'd earn a lot more with the seine-nets, surely? Those boats are more comfortable too and the work's not so hard . . . ?'

'We'd earn more for sure, but . . .' He didn't go on. He found it impossible to formulate his sense of loss, his passion for the kind of fishing where each man had his worth, before radar replaced native instinct, electronics bravery and experience.

'I've been after tuna since I was thirteen. Well, white tuna it was then. Bit different from the red . . .'

His kind of fishing might be done for but he wasn't beaten. And he was here to prove it. Might as well work on the factory boats. There was talk of using helicopters to track the flocks of birds gathered over the shoals of small fish which meant shoals of bigger fish below. Fishing grounds were expanding all the time. Already the north Atlantic had been cleaned out but here in Africa there were whole colonies of tuna waiting. His face lit up again. He wasn't bothered about 'the environment', which was just thought of as nature then. He liked to devastate. It was his job. He was, after all, a buccaneer, and the future was no concern of his.

It was one o'clock in the morning. Gavin gazed around him as if he had just returned to earth. George, half-asleep, lay curled in the crook of his arm. He had been talking to himself, almost, but he would never have dreamed of talking like that before now. Not to his wife. Not even to his brothers. He might have talked of plans, work and such, to his mates, but never of his feelings. That was woman-talk. What had come over him talking to her this way, about emotions and ideas he'd not known he had?

Gently he carried his mermaid to bed. 'Keep your foot up, else it'll make the blood run downwards to the sting. Now, I'm going to put on another cold compress for the night.'

George buried her face in his neck. It was the first time anyone had ever carried her like this, cared for her, in every sense of the word. She surrendered to this caring she had never known. Oh yes, once: her father, who had done a year at medical school before turning to art, had been a medical orderly during the war. He had hands that could clean wounds. Her mother hadn't been able to stand the sight of blood. The smell of iodine came back to her. 'it stings!' she always cried. 'All the better,' her father answered, 'It shows it's working.'

Tonight, for the first time, as they tenderly drifted to sleep, embraced, clinging like two children together, their minds were as closely bonded as their bodies.

The next morning George's foot was so much better that they decided to explore Praslin. Bicycling would have been too tiring for George, so they rented the one car on the island for a day. They looked at every cove but it was the smallest, Marie-Louise, which had the richest underwater treasures to offer, a stone's throw from the shore. No need to swim:

under three feet of water clear as glass lay a garden of marine plants, teeming with fish, through which Gavin and George glided, scarcely moving their flippers. It was just there that the explorers of the *Heureuse Marie* had found the coconut grove in the Vallée de Mai, which they were going to visit the next day. Not far, the buccaneer La Buse (whom the English call La Booze, because they can never manage the French u) had landed after seizing the most fabled booty in the history of piracy: the viceroy of India with his gold plate and the archbishop of Goa with his sacred vessels studded with precious stones . . . All this and more they learned as, stretched on the hot sand under the trees, far from the real world, they read the guide book together.

When they made love that afternoon they indulged in the first-time luxury of postponing orgasm. It was the first time, too, that Gavin felt he was surrendering to the woman he was taking, which moved him, made him shy. He allowed her to take 'it', as he called it, into her mouth, and let himself show the acute pleasure it gave him. He wouldn't come in her mouth though. It shamed him to do that. At the last moment he pulled her up to face him.

'I respect you too much for that. It's silly maybe, but I just couldn't do it, not in your mouth.'

'Trust me. I'm only doing what I want to do. I promise I'll stop if I don't like it. I never force myself with you.'

'Perhaps, but still I can't. You're not mad at me? He ran his tongue over her lips, as if washing away the touch of his penis. 'I feel all alone up here without you. It's so good when I can feel you all over. You're not mad at me, are you? Now this,' and he pushed himself smoothly into the place he had prepared, 'this is how I want to finish.' And her 'place' closed round him so that every curve, every in-and-out of their sleek bodies was complete, equal, fitted. He stayed motionless within her.

'You never said if you were mad at me.' What a hypocrite! Mad *for* him more likely, thought George.

'This is no time to say if I'd like it any other way. I want you so much I'll never get beyond the missionary position.'

He laughed, delighted. She laughed at delighting him. They laughed from childlike happiness at holding the secret to each other's pleasure, a secret one could live one's whole life without discovering.

Very gently he started to move inside her. For all the gravity of their desire they were still smiling as they kissed, their teeth clashing.

During the brief respites George would wonder how she could ever manage it again, especially as Gavin's equipment remained imposing even after use. She remarked on this as he wandered naked around their room.

'It just won't go down, not when you're around. Never completely. It's terrible!' He laughed boyishly. 'And the minute I start talking about it . . . well, just look.' He contemplated his organ with rueful indulgence, as if it were a naughty child. He was innocently proud of being admired. It was the one thing he wasn't prudish about: he knew, whatever else was wrong with him it wasn't his body.

'To think I've had to come all the way to the equator to see you walking around in a constant state of . . . abnormality? . . . animality?' She took his penis in her hand, weighing it. 'My god, even empty it must weigh, oh, let's see, half a pound at least!' She loved to flatter him, to say silly things, kneel before his wondrous tool like Lady Chatterley, of whom he had never heard. She loved to sweet-talk him into being even more aroused. In short, she liked to behave like a sex-object, give free rein to a salaciousness, a lewdness she hadn't known was in her. This was another of the reasons she loved Gavin. He revealed the unknown woman who leapt out and took her over. A creature, she became, who never read at night so as not to delay a moment's pleasure, who dressed according to his desires, who forgave all the crudities, the illiteracies she would have despised in anyone else, who did all this because of the outrageous pleasure he gave her, the crazy, inexcusable passion he woke in her. Why did it need to be excused anyway? Why this rage to quantify sex as if it were a science? Sex is simply sex.

George's internal critic, her mental chaperone, now reminded her how frivolous and inadvisable all this was, suggesting that it was only the exotic surroundings which kept this flame alight. That she and Gavin had never spent ten whole days together. On better acquaintance, the inevitable repetitiveness of love-making would become tedious, and would, hopefully end this obsession, leaving her with a genteel regret more compatible with the demands of their two lives. (*You could at least try to hold out for two hours without lusting for him,* said the chaperone. *Just look at the way you're eyeing him. I know what's on your dirty little mind.*' 'I just can't help it,' responded George to her alter ego. 'Even at night his slightest movement wakes me, and drowsiness naturally turns into sexiness, like those engravings where the bird's wing slowly turns into a sail and you can't spot exactly when the change began. Even first thing in the morning he has only to lay a finger on me, not necessarily on a volatile zone, for my breathing to become a groan of pleasure, for our mouths, our bodies, our sexes to join. *That's quite enough of that. It's always the same story with you. How tedious . . .*')

Each morning George woke with the fear that the chaperone might have succeeded in disciplining the joyous adolescent within her, the girl only Gavin knew. But each morning it was still the girl from Raguenès who shivered at the first touch of this man who always woke first, and would lie watching her sleep, resisting the urge to run his fingers lightly over the tip of her breast.

'Sailors don't know how to sleep in,' he'd apologise, his approaching hand signalling the daily defeat of the chaperone. A glorious defeat: the moment they realised that the whole day lay before them they went wild with joy and would make love two or three times non-stop. When they felt knocked out for the count, they made the resolution to have breakfast *first* but an accidental touch would fling them both back on the bed.

It was perhaps just as well then – for Gavin wasn't a man to make love out of doors – that they left their hut next day to explore the main island. In the evening they dined on seafood in a tiny restaurant between the beach and an unfrequented dirt road. The only sound came from a small native orchestra – violin, accordion, triangle and drums – which was playing minuets and quadrilles straight from the court of Louis XIV. The five ill-assorted musicians in their ragged trousers and tropical shirts accompanied the stately dance of an old Seychelles woman in a long skirt and with beautiful broad hard-working feet. There, under the plantains and palm trees, the airs of the Sun King were brought back to life as she danced with the dignity of a duchess. Toothless, a badly creased shawl over her thin shoulders, her skirt hem coming down, she glinted with mischief and good fun, as true and lovely as her island. Thanks to this little group, the epoch of the great explorers, before conquest was taken over by generals and tycoons, was rekindled for George and Gavin. Before long the old dancer would be replaced by some ghastly girl singer, the timeless musicians by electric guitars playing 'folk' music.

There were only six of them dining that night, and the other four – clearly a family party – were French too. They looked soulless. Ageless too. Already on the turn. The older woman was impeccable, her grey hair drawn into a chignon, straight-backed and with a square, distinguished, even handsome, face, which bore the marks of virtue too long practised. She was wearing a raw linen suit and the inevitable white sandals. Her husband, who could only have been a colonial administrator, sat abstracted, his head lowered, at the head of the table, glazed by thirty years of connubial tedium. Their daughter, likewise ageless, had dyed black hair with auburn highlights ('so much more flattering, don't you think?') and was partnered by a sorry specimen treading in his father-in-law's footsteps. The Tropics hadn't cracked their bourgeois carapaces. The two women scrutinised their plates for any sign of an indigenous germ, then frowned over the menu which offered only fish, before demanding toasted sandwiches.

It emerged that they were on their way back from the Vallée de Mai, and were already regretting having bought themselves a *coco-fesse*, one of those notorious double coconuts which look like the hips and pudenda of a woman. It had cost the earth, and now they were beginning to see how obscene it was. They would never dare exhibit it in their drawing-room. The mother and daughter were the only ones making conversation, and then only sporadically. The men just nodded from time to time.

'That terribly pleasant hotel on Lake Garda . . . Mama, you know the one I mean?'

'Oh yes, don't you remember, Henri?' Madame addressed her husband with the formal '*vous*'. His attitude showed the boredom of thirty years of conjugal holidays in the company of his wife which now, with his retirement, had become one interminable holiday. But he wouldn't stick it to the end: already he had furnished himself with a precautionary heart attack and was functioning only intermittently, on three cylinders.

Six French people finding themselves together six thousand miles from home and more than five hundred from Madagascar, the nearest landfall, couldn't simply ignore one another. They made acquaintance over the *coco-fesse*.

'Nowadays every single one is numbered, you know,' observed Madame Mère. 'Only a certain quantity can be exported each year.'

'Isn't it odd that this is the one place where they grow?' said George. 'Arab princes used to pay enormous sums for them, because of their aphrodisiac properties.'

Reprobation passed fleetingly over Madame Mère's face. Was she being suspected of erotic tendencies? Gavin raised an interested eyebrow. He might not know about the goddess Aphrodite, but the word 'aphrodisiac' meant something.

'Funny they should need it, those Arab princes. They could have their pick of any woman they wanted.'

The conversation was taking a disturbing turn for the two ladies, who changed the subject to something more decorous.

'Don't these islands have the most heavenly names?'

'Yes,' George agreed. 'It's moving to hear the name of Louis XVI's minister all the time, when he never actually set foot here.'

'Why Praslin anyway?' asked Gavin. George knew perfectly well that he didn't give a damn but she was going to

97

tell him all the same since she had read it up in the *Guide Bleu* that very day.

'Because the Duc de Praslin was Naval Minister then, and financed a voyage specifically to get hold of these infamous *coco-fesses*. They cost the earth even then.'

'At least', remarked Monsieur Père, 'there weren't any natives living on the islands then. Saved Praslin's men from being cannibalised like poor Lapérouse.'

'And Séchelles himself never set foot here.' Monsieur the son-in-law lectured. 'Minister of Finance, that's who he was, Moreau de Séchelles, to give him his full name. I'm an Inspector of Finance myself,' he added complacently.

'It's a lovely name. If it had been the British we'd have had to put up with New South Wales or South Liverpool.' Being so far from home brought out unexpected patriotism in George, making her happy to inveigh against perfidious Albion.

Gavin caught George's eye. He had a sharp ear for a pun and, in French, 'Liverpool' – '*L'Hiver-poule*' – sounds like 'winter whore'.

The French family didn't want to pursue the conversation, unable to place this unlikely couple in their bourgeois scheme of things. All four bade goodnight with wintry smiles, and made for Praslin's only hotel.

'Don't, whatever you do, buy us a *coco-fesse*,' said George. 'Don't even touch one. It would finish us off.'

Next day they took a boat to the neighbouring island of La Digue. Time was slipping away, and this was to be their last port of call. After a half an hour crossing in the rain, the old schooner *Belle Coraline* pulled in at a rickety jetty on stilts. It was still raining. It was always raining somewhere on these islands, but they had spent the whole time on deck, sprayed by waves and downpours, childish with love.

La Digue had neither village nor harbour, just a few scattered one-storey houses, a copra mill still turned by an ox, a Catholic church and a neglected cemetery where the gravestones had French names. An ox-cart took them to Gregory's Lodge, a cluster of bungalows which made up the one hotel on this island of four cars and two thousand inhabitants. The dripping foliage made constant plopping sounds, the sheets were damp, and every night a symphony of frogs, insects and birds, interrupted from time to time by a harsh cry, accompanied the ceaseless rustling of palm trees and made sleep impossible. At that season the dirt tracks became streams of mud, and the breakers brought in piles of pungent seaweed, reminding them of Raguenès. But on the lee shore, beyond the pink granite screes of this tropical Brittany, there were secret beaches of unbearable whiteness, shaded by coconut palms and bordered by lagoons the colour of absinthe.

The evenings were perfect: the wind died down at sunset, and there was an hour of peace before the nightly cacophony. Then, with their 'perked-up' fruit juice, as Gavin called it, adding a generous measure of gin, they recalled their childhoods, so geographically close, so socially distant, and the people of Raguenès, his village, which had been her village too for the summers. It was odd how they could be talking about the same people, the same landscapes, yet have such different versions.

They hired bicycles and explored the island as far as Patate Cove with its haphazard clutter of granite rocks and enormous, deafening breakers. In the evening, they walked one last time along the shining edge of the sea, baring their skins to the almost liquid wind, before making for their bed, a boat anchored at the sea's edge, among the swishing and crashing sounds of the ocean.

Conan came to collect them and sail them back to Mahé. Their last night was spent in the Hotel Louis XVII, where, their landlady recounted – for the thousandth time – the legend of the little Capet, Louis XVI's son, who had arrived there with a store of plate engraved with the Bourbon crest and, under the name of Pierre-Louis Poiret, had lived the rest of his life on that very spot.

They were to part next day, and for them parting meant losing each other, perhaps for ever. They had parted 'for ever' once or twice already. Hoping – vainly – to fill up on him as provision, George wanted to make demands that night, direct his love-making until she had reached the exact moment. Usually she preferred him to take the initiative, even though he often thought she was ready before she actually was, and proceeded to the next phase. Not much too soon, just enough to add a spice of frustration. She preferred her ecstasy tinged with frustration. The special value of pleasure seemed its precariousness. And it was so moving when – frowning with concentration, eyes ferocious as if he were about to tackle Everest – Gavin decided that it was his turn and raised himself on his knees, pulling her to him fiercely determined. Then, sitting, they would make love face to face, gazing into each other's eyes until they could bear it no longer.

That night she had no need to hold him to her after their love-making. For once he lay by her, in the tender redolence of their love, without his habitual dash to wash off its traces. No doubt Marie-Josée disapproved of love's effusions. For her, fornication once over, you should wash, get dressed and decent enough to look the children in the eye. Gavin was astonished that George, far from being disgusted by his semen, complained that his rush for the shower made her feel lonely and neglected. She wasn't going to wash straight away, if only to break with the squalid ritual of her young days, when every second's delay increased the danger of conception, and no amount of cologne in the place of perdition could guarantee impunity. So they lay entwined, careful not to talk about the future.

That future was to send them in opposite directions the next day. George would write to him, *poste restante*, at Pointe Noire. If all went well he would write back once a fortnight when he came ashore. To say what, though? 'Dear Madame, the wind's been strong'? It's a sad business, loving a cormorant. But at least these southern seas were less dangerous than the north Atlantic.

In the fifteen hours her journey took, George would just get herself together, restore everything to its rightful place. Her sex, for a start. Yes. It's you I'm talking to, cunt of mine. You're going to have some rest at last. God knows you need it, chum. For ten days you've been unremittingly disturbed, ploughed, assaulted, fulfilled. But you were always prepared like the good little scout you are. You made an utter slave of me, and you had me fooled. It's funny, the strangers one harbours within one. But it's not right that they should always be in charge.

The party's over, chum.

6
Danger Signals

Tell me that I would soon have got over it if we had lived together, Gavin and I. Tell me that we mustn't wreck our lives, especially not him.

Tell me that it's madness to trust what the body tells one, that its messages are fickle and can lead to crazy decisions which soon could prove disastrous.

Tell me that if I want to keep this love of mine I must accept losing it.

Tell me all this because, for the time being, I've lost my bearings. I'm existing on the margin of life, in a decompression chamber where I'm trying to detoxify myself from the delicious drug of being adored. When I finally surface I shall have to reacquaint myself with Sidney's well-tuned love-making, his narrow shoulders, premature stoop and nonchalance, while the feel of Gavin's dense muscles is still on my palms, his energy still surrounds me. Like a girl, I'm carrying his first love letter around with me. It's a small sheet of paper he slipped to me at the airport 'for when you've left my life again'. I was terribly touched, not just by what he wrote, but by the laborious handwriting and careful spelling of a good schoolboy. 'Before, it seemed like all days were the same, and that's how it would be until I died. But since you – don't ask me to explain. All I know is that I want to hold you in my life. And in my arms sometimes, if that's what you want too. You said that what's happened to us is like a sickness. If it is I don't want to get better ever. The idea that somewhere in the world you are living, that you think of me sometimes, helps me to go on living.'

Luckily I knew Gavin too well, or at least thought I did, to worry that a grand passion could detract for long from his love of his job which was his very taste for life. The sea would regain its hold, would give him back the sense of his true values, would perhaps even make him hate me for a time for causing him to swerve from his proper course. If that would help him that's how I wanted it: I felt it was I who gained most in this relationship, and was therefore the guiltier one. Our situation caused me much less pain, and gave me so much more enjoyment, because its incongruity gave me pleasure without remorse.

Sidney knew nothing about it, or only very little. I didn't want to offer up Gavin as fodder for his irony. They were no match for each other, and I might have been tempted to betray my cormorant if I had tried to describe what he was to Sidney, for whom the intellect was pre-eminent, even in a love affair. He would have pointed out that I was doing a Lady Chatterley, and congratulated me on engaging in a very chic experiment. So, partly out of cowardice and partly to spare Sidney's self-esteem, I did not try to explain what it was that linked me so deeply to Lozerech. I couldn't explain it even to myself. I may be a rotten liar, but I do have a certain talent for omission.

The only people I told were Frédérique and François. My sister was starting to wonder what I could still get out of this endless soap opera, and suggested that I try a change of scenery. Frédérique is a sentimental but earnest soul, married to a nice, foolish ecologist with a beard. Of course. Fanatical about camping, rock-climbing and hiking, which all meant early nights, a 'quickie' with his wife on Sunday mornings before he hied himself off to play football with his friends. At least, that's how I imagined their sex life, a suspicion confirmed by the slightly pinched look on my sister's face when I described my guilty goings-on. I secretly hoped that my adventures would turn her thoughts to the divorce I felt she must get if she were ever to live her life to the full.

'When I think how you used to tease me about Frédéric with a q-u-e! Now you're the George who enjoys a roll in the Sand,' she mocked, reverting to the word games and puns of our childhood.

Unlike my sister, François thought that what I had with Gavin was too much the stuff of high romance to be ranked with ordinary adultery. Each time I returned from one of my trysts he would want to know about my feelings. He was someone I could talk completely freely with: a former boyfriend, constant in his friendship and a doctor too, he was one of those rare men who had all the female qualities. An exceptional combination, François.

I didn't talk about it with my American friends, except for Ellen, always avid to hear about such exploits which, invariably, she put down to sex and nothing but sex. She said she could see from my expression and the way I moved that I had been 'fucked out of my brain': 'No mistaking that inane look on your face and that swing of the ass.' How could I convince her that, yes, it was sex which attracted me to Gavin but, at the same time, so much more than sex.

And yet, it was nice to be back with Sidney and, in some ways, actually a relief. I wanted us to read the papers in bed together, to discuss world politics, to resume our squabbles about art and literature. I had missed his ironic humour, and the way we understood each other without having to spell everything out. With him I was on my own territory again, the world of dons and intellectuals, who analysed their lives even as they lived them, endlessly debating and theorising, 'calling themselves into question', as they put it. Gavin loved a good laugh but wit made him uncomfortable, and it would never have occurred to him to stand far enough from his life to analyse it. He functioned as a wolf does, and never dreamt of being anything other than a wolf. He hunted to survive, and if he found a savage pleasure in the hunt that was an extra; he would have functioned in the same way if it had offered only pain. There was no ambiguity about his life's purpose: it was simply to provide for his female and his young. His work was sacred since that was his fate as a wolf. He had swerved from his path only once, for my sake and for the sake of things which normally he considered worthless: pleasure, an inexplicable attraction. The lures of Satan, were these not?

As for me, I was amazed by how mute my body had become after its clamorousness with Gavin, like not being able to face the thought of drink after a bender. Now I wondered how on earth I could have allowed myself to carry on like a sex-maniac and feel so happy about it. I wasn't very demanding with Sidney at this time, but we were both so busy he didn't seem to notice. That July I was due to return to France permanently, and he had decided to take a sabbatical year and accompany me. This entailed finding somewhere to live, getting Loïc into a *lycée*, packing up everything I had accumulated over ten years and last but, in the States, far from least, saying goodbye to all our friends. We went from party to party, finishing up depressed by the repeated farewells. But these were inevitable rituals: in a nation where culture is thin on the ground, the little band of scholars and teachers establish powerful bonds of friendship and solidarity, like freemasonry or a loving but demanding family, touchy but conformist.

I was looking forward to returning to the individualism of the French, their unconcern, their lack of civic spirit and their skill at turning professional rivalries into an art form. The only two people I would miss were Ellen Price and her husband Alan, both professors at NYU; Ellen especially, with her competence and pragmatism and that business sense, which even academics respect in the States. What's more, she was a true American beauty, by which I mean a beauty of such flawlessness as to seem unreal. With her blonde hair and blue eyes, she had that milk-fed, corn-fed, steak-fed air. Vitaminised and psychoanalysed to the core, she saw comfort and health as her right, and unhappiness as an illness. A pure product of American technology, in short. For two years she had been working on a book about women's sexuality which had the bald title *Orgasm*. Her post at NYU absolved her work from any taint of pornography, while the new discipline of Women's Studies gave her the authority to send out breathtakingly detailed and impertinent questionnaires and even to get a grant for her research, something which would have been unthinkable in France. 'Orgasm' was a word which still had the power to shock the French in 1965, but in the USA it was endowed with scientific significance. Sure that I had a problem – for her everything was a problem, to be cured or resolved – she let me see the first draft of her book, convinced that it would teach me how to achieve full orgasm with Gavin. 'You must check everything's OK in that department,' she would decree earnestly. (She used 'OK' all the time. In America it can mean anything: yes, maybe, fine, lovely weather, piss off, perhaps, see you.) She saw herself as the first genuine explorer of the dark continent of sex,

Kinsey, according to Ellen, having propounded far too statistically oriented a view of female sexuality. As for male sexuality, she announced in a lecture to her dumbfounded colleagues that it was so primitive it merited no more than ten pages in any book.

I hoped at least to find the answer to that question which every woman asks herself: whether I came properly. Her definition was brazenly assured: 'Orgasm is a great wave which originates in the toes.' Good heavens! *My* wave originates in the rude bits and my coccyx, and it's there that it gathers and breaks, depriving my noble bits of a role and reducing my mind to thinking about nothing but sensations. Even when my breasts are caressed, something which always sets the 'shameful' process going, I feel the vibration below, 'down under', as they say in Australia. Not in my toes, though.

'You ought to be pleased,' said Ellen. 'It shows you belong to the sixty per cent of women whose nipples are erogenous.'

The word 'nipple', of course, is anything but erogenous. Mind you , 'teat' or 'tit' – associated with babies and birds – aren't much better. Ellen also informed me that only ten or fifteen per cent of men have sexually sensitive nipples. Well! poor them. But she was quite unable to explain how it operated, this wave of hers, which flows down from the breasts to the genitals. Along a naughty nerve, perhaps? Or by a hermetic line, as in acupuncture? A mental trajectory? I'd say that where sex is concerned, *tout fait ventre*, everything starts in the belly, as the French so neatly put it!

At least her book reassured me about the notorious female ejaculation, about which de Sade and others had given me such an inferiority complex with their rhapsodies about furious discharges, inexhaustible fountains, wells of nectar.

Gosh! did that mean that I, and the few women friends I dared to ask, were sexual cripples? Not at all said Ellen's book: 'Research has shown that this phenomenon is extremely rare, and then only sporadic.' Thank goodness for that! 'Except for a handful of extreme cases involving the Skene glands there is nothing in that region capable of producing an appreciable amount of fluid,' she herself added in the brisk tones of a surgeon who cuts through vaginas the way geologists cut through rock strata.

One final anxiety: those three-inch clitorises described by pornographers and a few ethnologists. 'Pure male fantasy,' she asserted. 'Total ignorance about the female anatomy and the mechanisms of tumescence.' Phew! *That's* all right then.

And yet Ellen's research had no explanation to offer on the tumescence of the heart. It was more like a cook book or a DIY manual than a discourse on pleasure. I didn't dare point out to her that John Cowper Powys or Wilhelm Reich had explained and validated pleasure, all pleasure, without falling into her sexual Stakhanovism. As soon as I got back from my trip with Lozerech she asked me how many orgasms I had had. She couldn't believe I hadn't made notes, pitying me as I tried to explain that my data might be a bit blurred, and that I often enjoyed the slalom leading to the finishing post as much as the finish itself. It's that virtually unpredictable, wayward course which takes you gasping, imploring or frantic, up to the final moment, which makes mutual sex so much better than masturbation. Solitary pleasure you can be sure of every time. It takes minimum effort, plus a few shop-soiled fantasies you'd never dare admit to having.

The only conclusion, I suppose, is that it's not possible to describe passion scientifically, that a rose is not a rose is not a rose. God, it's wonderful though, whatever Ellen thinks.

It's always dangerous to transplant a love which is past its first bloom. Back in France I couldn't help seeing Sidney in a different light. In the States he had been, with Loïc, integral to my life, a warm vital element. Now I was back with my family, my friends, my beloved French authors and French newspapers with their French gossip, so much more fascinating to me than Lana Turner's divorce or Elvis's weight problems or Sinatra's dodgy deals. I was starting to see Sidney as a midwestern hick, which was grossly unfair, as he had joyously immersed himself in our recent phenomenon, the *nouveau roman*. His only quibble was that *roman* sounded too like romance for his rarefied taste. At last he was living in the birthplace of what had, for him, rendered all previous fictional forms obsolete, breathing the air of the *nouveau roman*, meeting the authors. I suspect he was a bit disappointed to find that they were just like everyone else, blithe extroverts or boring theoreticians, flaunting no distinctive marks or way of dressing. He was planning to devote the entire year to the novel he had been nurturing for two years, which would be worthy of its models, since he aimed to take from it every spark of life which might make it the least like a romantic novel. For some years now, with the connivance of his fellow-academics, Sidney had sheltered behind a comforting contempt for any book which achieved popular success. He and his fellows admired only novels of mind-numbing tedium and infinitesimal sales, the epitome of which was a recent structuralist novel whose hero bore the name 'Structure', to make sure no one missed the point. I had started out reading it with the greatest goodwill, which dwindled steadily as I proceeded, until it became just an iron will to force myself on to the last page.

Was I perhaps indirectly influenced by Gavin? I no longer

believed in Sidney's sincerity or spontaneity when he tried to justify his novel being so dry, so without any kind of characterisation or action, as a quest for literary purity. All I could see in it was overwhelming greyness. Either I was irredeemably stupid or Sidney and his acolytes were clowns. Very serious clowns, mind you, who forgave my lack of enthusiasm. I was, after all, only an historian.

That year we had only a fortnight's holiday with Frédérique in Brittany. I was preparing the lectures I would be giving in Paris when the university year started, as well as working on a book commissioned by some academic publishers, expanding my thesis on women and revolutions. If Gavin and I met by chance in Raguenès we would exchange polite phrases. Our eyes alone reassured us that we really were the two people who, at different times, in different places, had made love so well, and, throughout the long winter, exchanged letters rather less 'polite' than our phrases in the village street. For we had gone on writing. Gavin posted his little notes from Pointe Noire every three or four weeks, when his ship put in for supplies or to unload its cargo of fish. I wrote, *poste restante*, letters which never caught up with his, pen strokes on water, vain attempts to reach a cormorant constantly hunting the deep. A correspondence which underlined the strangeness of our relationship. Gavin had left no recognisable marks on my life, knew nothing of the various places I had lived, except for my childhood home. He was only my dream life, and I wrote to him from a place where everything is possible and nothing is real. But our letters were very important to me. Even for someone like Gavin, who thought letters were only for basic information, the act of writing did something. Gently I mined his foundations, disturbing him only enough to rouse him to this form of pleasure which, for the moment, was the only one we could have.

We planned to meet in Casamance for a week or two at the end of the tuna season, before he returned to his family at Larmor. The obligation to meet so far from our usual world added spice for me, an escape from reality, which was doubtless the reason our relationship survived.

The rendezvous was fixed for the end of April in Dakar, and we would travel to Casamance where Gavin had rented a boat. But, on 2 April, Marie-Josée and their youngest son, Joël, were in a serious car crash on the Concarneau road, and the boy's skull was fractured. He was taken in a coma to the hospital at Rennes. Gavin telephoned me in Paris. As usual he said nothing about his own feelings, simply that we could not go away together now, but adding 'just yet'. Obviously he would have to spend the whole of his three-month leave at Larmor. 'I'll write,' he added as he hung up. It costs a lot to make a call from Senegal.

Perhaps it was because of the disembodied nature of our love that the disappointments and griefs of my dreaming life didn't impinge on my real life. It must be confessed too that it was a relief to be able to spend the Easter holidays with Loïc. An affair is lived at the expense of maternal and professional obligations, which means you feel permanently guilty. I hadn't yet said anything to Sidney. There are some advantages in being cowardly . . .

The change of plan also meant that I could meet Ellen when she arrived in France, more than ever the orgasmologist. Her book was a huge success in the States, but her marriage was on the rocks. A husband often finds it hard to cope with his wife's success, and this was aggravated in Al's case by the fact that Ellen's success came from a book about sex, teeming with anecdotes in which his phallus rarely figured heroically. He was aware of everyone's unspoken questions, pitying or prurient, about whether he went in for the Chinese Tourniquet or the Accelerated Wrist Vibrato or engaged in the Pelvic Floor Manoeuvre (on page 74) with Ellen.

Since the recent publication of the Kinsey Report, orgasm had started to be a fashionable topic in France, and Ellen was hoping that her book would be translated in its wake. She rushed between radio stations, women's magazines and newspapers, and the book's explicitness, her own blend of naïveté and cynicism, her accent and the doll-like innocence of her face caused a sensation. She set up discussion evenings at our house, hoping to add a chapter on the Latino-Christian orgasm. Since this approach often proved a positive incitement to high jinks, she had a good opportunity for some important practical studies in which she magnanimously offered to include Sidney and me. But I recognised wistfully, that my body was still too suffused with Gavin for me to take part in these frolics.

And there had been no letter from my cormorant since his wife's accident, no doubt his way of punishing himself. He was like a tribesman needing an expiatory rite, believing in some divine profit-and-loss account which would have to be settled one day. That day had come for him, and anyway he was always for paying for one's sins. Fate was battering him the way it always does those who offer themselves up for punishment, who feel they have no right to happiness. Unhappiness was Lozerech's norm.

Marie-Josée had been allowed home, but had to stay in bed, encased in plaster for some weeks. Joël, the boy, was out of danger, but there was some brain damage which could mean that he would not be able to live a normal life.

Marie-Josée's mother arrived, blind husband in tow, and installed herself to look after her daughter. They were never to leave again. The family, Brittany, adversity had all closed round Gavin, a stockade through which my words could not reach him.

There were four months of silence until, just before he set off for Africa again, he sent a note, asking me to forgive him for not knowing how to be selfish. Seeing his small, careful writing on the cheap brown envelope moved me more than I would have wished. '*Karedig*,' he wrote on his habitual small sheet of lined paper from the village grocery shop, 'I want you to know that you're everything that's best in my life. Every time we meet I think it's maybe the end of the road for us. You know what a bloody fatalist I am, but then life hasn't done me any favours. Sometimes I wonder how it would have been if what your parents thought and you not wanting to trust me then hadn't put us where we are now. Keep a corner of your heart for me. And I, well . . . "*Me ho Kar*." Look it up in your Breton dictionary. And that's how I'll always feel. But fate's against it.'

I didn't reply since he hadn't even said whether he would be going to the *poste restante* for letters. Besides, it seemed so unfair to encourage him to love me: how could I demand a love which made him sick with remorse, when for me it was an extra reason for living? Months passed, and I found myself focusing some of what I had been saving for Gavin on Sidney. Often you keep the best part of yourself for escapades, unwilling though I was to confess it. Sidney and I started working together again, translating his novel which Stock planned to publish in the spring. He wasn't expecting much success, only the esteem of his friends and the few critics he admired. Or so he told himself.

As well as my new work, I had the business of helping Loïc readjust to a country he no longer thought of as home. A child can't live in the States for ten years, at the time when he's forming his loves, hates and ideas, without becoming something of a little American. Luckily I had Jean-Christophe's support in this. My ex-husband had two daughters by his new wife, a secret disappointment, so his son became more important for him. Through Loïc we were able to meet without bitterness or rancour, in that affectionate indifference which exists only between exes. I realised I could get on well with him now. Only when a man doesn't impress you any longer do you know how to manage him, only when you've fallen out of love can you make him fall in love with you.

I was getting to that stage with Sidney too, a becalmed, tranquil zone. But ought tranquillity to be the highest good for a thirty-five-year-old? Well, yes, perhaps, if I thought about Ellen and Al in the process of divorcing, she with gusto, he with bitterness and self-loathing. Yes, if I thought about that devoted couple, François and Luce, into whose lives trouble had come in the shape of a tiny lump on Luce's left breast. Yes, if I thought of the terrible chain which, from now on, bound Lozerech to a wife broken by the cruel handicap of their child.

Yes, certainly, compared with these, the affectionate, passionless equilibrium I shared with Sidney had to be considered happiness.

7
Disney World

Sometimes, years can pass for certain lovers without their ever becoming strangers to one another. The instant they saw each other again, Gavin and George knew with complete certainty that the three previous years, made up of so many weeks and months, were no more than a long interval between acts. This time it was he who broke the silence. Returning from a harder expedition than usual, in that far-away Africa where he felt so remote from his roots, from Finistère's soft rain and the smell of his own sea, so bereft of family, friends and the warmth of his own home, he felt the sudden need to bewail his solitude. And, though what he called 'being down' shamed him, who better to talk about it to than the person who had listened so well before?

The letter was only two pages to say things weren't going too well, but a man just had to get on with it, that the fishing had been bad that winter, and that he might as well go back to planting potatoes if all he got for his back-breaking work was peanuts.

Things weren't going too well for George either, lovewise. So it took only a few letters to rekindle their longing to see each other again, to sleep together, to appease each other's need, even if only for a few days.

The problem was that Gavin couldn't contemplate taking the money he needed for an illicit holiday from the meagre profits of that winter's fishing. George had some money that year, but only after protracted negotiations did she persuade him to accept a 'loan' for his air ticket to Jamaica, where Ellen had offered them the use of her apartment. He insisted on repaying it in monthly instalments, unable to bear being, as he solemnly put it, 'kept by a woman'.

Gavin didn't have the time, the imagination or the network of friends needed to mount this kind of clandestine operation, so George undertook the elaborate planning required to bring them to Miami airport within a few hours of each other – he from Africa, she from Montreal, where she had been giving a series of lectures. George was the first to arrive. Pacing up and down before the arrivals gate where he should soon appear if everything went as planned, she wondered for the thousandth time what power it was that ruled them. '*It's your cunt,*' said her chaperone. 'Sure,' retorted George, 'but why mine in particular? There are plenty of them about, in Europe as well as Africa, a quim for every whim.' As life went on – and George was now almost thirty-eight – she saw, more and more, that what she had with Gavin was unique. She had been through various love affairs, fleeting or serious, encountering male sexual organs limited in appeal by their owners, by the brains behind or rather above them. She had found that penises cannot be reduced to the level of their masters. The witty intellectual could turn out to be no more than a road drill, the Don Juan an idolater of his own prick, while a simple peasant might have the delicacy of a goldsmith.

It was that goldsmith for whom she was waiting. It was with him she would take a charter flight to Kingston where they were to spend ten days in Ellen's studio apartment. Like many of their colleagues in the United States and Canada, Ellen and Al had some years earlier bought themselves a holiday 'hole' at the Montego Beach Club. It was in a vast, semi-luxurious condominium, with a balcony high above an equally vast beach. 'Just what you need. I use it myself in similar situations,' announced Ellen, always more than happy to promote adultery.

But a few hours later George almost lost her nerve. It loomed over them, a huge concrete rabbit warren, one of a cliff of similarly daunting apartment blocks. How was she going to spend ten days there with no resources apart from 'I'm horny, you're horny'? Wouldn't Gavin resent getting into debt for this? Mightn't they be disappointed in each other? That day would undoubtedly come. At thirty-eight you're beginning to worry about the body's imperfections, scrutinising your women friends, trying to find out what goes on sexually nowadays, what men are looking for in bed, what women do.

These schoolgirlish anxieties had driven George to watch a blue movie for the first time in her life. She was emboldened by being so far from home – in Quebec where she lectured for a month each year in the Women's Studies department of Laval University. She came out of the cinema dismayed. Seen like that on a giant screen, surrounded by chortling friends, the monotonous heavings had seemed sleazy and cheap, sexual activity ludicrous. That was what sex would seem when she was old, which she was soon to be. She hoped at least that it would seem ludicrous. Otherwise how could one bear being too old for it?

Already she was at an age when a long flight on top of a month's intensive work in the harsh climate of Canada had taken its toll. To cap it all, during the flight she had read a magazine survey on the poor opinion women had of their own genitals: forty per cent of the respondents had classified their vaginas as 'rather ugly'. How would Gavin find hers? *Was* there such a thing as a pretty cunt, charming objectively, that is, and not just in the besotted eyes of sweet, adoring fools? George had always worried about what her North American friends called her 'beaver', suspecting that a love affair could never survive a close scrutiny of that area. Those professional cunt-scrutinisers, the erotic writers, confirmed her worst fears and threatened her sexual confidence. Even the most highly respected of these writers, Calaferte for instance, were part of a foul conspiracy to make women resign themselves to the dreadful abjection of their sex. How could you rejoice in owning 'a mindless gash enfolding a coil of tentacles dotted with flaccid suction cups and bristling with tiny nails and knives . . . and invisible gelatinous hooks'? How could you permit a poor innocent who had never read these authors to see your 'uterine frenzy, unsatisfied by even the most prodigious phallus', your 'gaping hole, suppurating and filthy'? All a woman could do, confronted by the 'scarlet torch' and the 'divine spur', described by the same authors, was wallow in shame. Fearing that her flaccid suction cups or gelatinous hooks might be showing, George had always kept her thighs clamped together whenever a man's glance lingered on her body.

Mind you, male equipment was pretty funny, with that swinging trunk and two old pouches, wrinkled from birth. But men had always known how to promote that stupefying trio. Women had missed out on selling themselves. Even now George was not accustomed to the sea anemone between her legs, with its rosy, inert volutes which aspired to be the site of ecstasies so glorious that a man would travel three thousand miles for them. There had to be some misunderstanding.

She was painfully convinced that Gavin must feel the same way: he had made no attempt to kiss her, either in the plane or in the airport bus, or now, in the apartment. They chattered inconsequentially as they unpacked, to hide their discomfort and, as the moment of truth approached, he suggested a swim before dinner.

'I've got much better at it, you'll see,' he said. Just before they went out he solemnly produced a large parcel from his case.

'Have a look at this. I chose it for you. Sorry I didn't have any nice paper for it.'

She was always wary when she opened these brown paper parcels of his, not being a good soul able to hide her dismay at her cormorant's various finds. Today's was the worst of the lot. She just managed to repress a scream of horror at the mother-of-pearl sunset, the tinted coral palm trees and the girls in fluorescent grass skirts, all lit from behind by a bulb which made the sky glow red. God almighty! It was a mercy Gavin never came to her house, and wouldn't discover his picture lying in the bottom of her wardrobe, her Chamber of Horrors. It already contained the coconut-shell dancer (his first gift), a camel-skin handbag with a bright orange lining in rayon satin and a Moroccan cushion embroidered with their birth signs, Aquarius and Aries.

George kissed him so as to regain her composure, hide her shudder at the thought of Sidney coming upon this hair-raising work of art in her suitcase. Gavin contemplated it lovingly before re-wrapping it and – you can never be too careful – locking it into the Louis XV reproduction Formica closet. George shut the multicoloured plastic blinds and, enjoined by notices on every door of their love nest, No. 1718, triple-locked the front door. My god, if Sidney could see her in this setting, comic in its pure functionalism, with this diffident-looking bloke, he would be seized with endless glee. Sidney's mirth was rarely without malice.

But the warm, tropical sea, good girl that it is, dispersed the clouds of the journey, indeed of their separation, which had been too long. Freed from winter clothes, they could rediscover the familiar landscape of each other's bodies. But they were strangers still. They decided to eat in a restaurant their first evening. At the Kalabasha there were tables at the water's edge, attentive service and soft music to compensate for the vile Jamaican wine, both tasteless and acid, and local crayfish whose flavour couldn't compare with the Breton ones, or even the Mauretanian green variety. George and Gavin pretended to be tourists who had just met on the plane.

'You like the sea?'

'Never really thought about it. Got no choice, seeing as I'm a fisherman and all.'

A man who could come out with phrases like this needed to be handsome for George to fancy him. But handsome he was, with a lover's handsomeness, glorious in a way you never found in the groves of academe, handsome like Hugo's *Travailleur de la mer*.

'And what brings you to Jamaica?'

'Good question. Can't rightly say. I only just got here.'

'And you don't know anyone here? That's a shame, a handsome boy like you. Let's see, perhaps I have a friend . . .'

Gavin looked uncertain. Teasing flummoxed him and, except in bed, compliments made him uncomfortable. But the band came to their rescue, and they made their way to the dance floor. The West Indian music was served up in an American sauce, so as not to startle the tourists, music having become political these days. George was wearing a low-cut black top with a lace border. She did not usually wear either black or lace, but then she didn't usually dine in Jamaica with a Breton fisherman. The lace was a bit tarty, but it felt right for the occasion.

They had been apart for so long that they had forgotten their private vocabulary. It was all ridiculous and exciting. They walked slowly back to the condo along the seafront. All the gift shops and supermarkets were dark, only the sea shone quietly to itself. Gavin and George began to cope with the situation.

'I live there,' said George. 'The seventeenth floor. Would you like to come up for a drink?'

They gazed up at the monstrous hive. Every cell had its couple, legitimate no doubt, since this was an American enclave. Each balcony had its man, tinkling ice-cubes in the rum punch he hoped would rekindle waning ardour for his immaculately coiffed and deodorised wife.

At last, Gavin became crude in the elevator. Looking round him innocently, he pressed his bulging crotch to George's hip. Her hand brushed over it as if by accident. As hand greeted cock ('Hello, pleased to meet you'), she wondered why they hadn't started that way. Their bodies had always known how to converse. The other couples in the elevator hadn't noticed a thing. They were sailing up to their cells, surrounded by syrupy music and posters promising them the ecstasy of a natural paradise ('Laze on a tropical island and breathe an air heavy with perfumes . . . Nature, freedom, and all the luxury you could wish').

They made for the balcony, to lean over its dizzy height, like the twelve hundred other couples, gazing down at the almost deserted beach. There were only a few Jamaicans in orange uniforms there, collecting the plastic wrappers, beer cans and empty bottles of sun lotion. So much for the relative 'ecstasy' of a natural paradise.

George began to feel that this package holiday would give her perverse pleasure. It was so different from the cultural trips in uncomfortable coaches organised by Sidney, she revelled in its vulgar charm. Better than a tour in Berri with the George Sand Society, or the Treasures of Bruges with a lecturer from the Louvre – Departures every Sunday at 6 a.m., Place de la Concorde. Nothing could spoil the joy spreading within her; everything conspired to increase it. Why was real life so complicated?

Almost before they had reached the sitting room Gavin put his lips to her cleavage. The black lace had worked after all. He slid his finger under the bra strap down to her breast. Sneaky manoeuvre. That was her weak spot and he knew it. She struggled for self-control. It wouldn't be playing the game if they undressed straight away. God knows, they had waited for three years, and still had ten days in which to carry on like beasts. Tonight was for courtly love, the lady and the knight.

'What can I offer you?' she asked him.

'You. On toast.'

'*Oh no!*' screamed the chaperone. '*That's not even worthy of bad vaudeville.*' 'But that's why I love him,' said George. 'I could never play-act with anyone else like this. So clear off, will you?' '*And this place, for heaven's sake,*' the chaperone went on. '*Have you looked at it? Straight from a B-movie, where the cowman seduces the lady of the manor.*' 'Cowboy, if you don't mind, at least on this side of the Atlantic. "*Same difference. Your cowboy's got a hard-on like a bull. If I'm not mistaken, it'll be in you in five minutes, my girl.*'

'You can't take one breast out and leave the other in the dark.' George simpered, ignoring the chaperone's contemptuous remarks. He stroked one hand over her skirt, right on her magnetic centre, the other struggled with her bra fastening. 'Why do you wear this thing? You don't need it with breasts like yours.'

'It makes undressing last longer.'

She drew away to switch off the red lantern on the balcony, then returned to unzip the jeans of this guy she had met on the plane. Even with his trousers round his ankles, his beautiful thighs saved him from looking ridiculous. Years in the south Atlantic had tanned his chest, and that brown, baby-smooth skin under its covering of hair . . . well . . . Forget courtly love, forget the chaste lady and the knight . . . now she was a sea anemone, swaying in the current. Come on, handsome stranger. Show me how you make love. It's been so long I've almost forgotten.

('Yes, you're right, chaperone, that dark ivory thing of his with its helmet top, well, he's going to put it into me. And, you see, just now, nothing seems more beautiful in creation than to open myself to this man and, when he's deep inside, to close around him. Right to the end of the world, tra-la, right to the end of the world.')

They had not even kissed yet, though their eyes were fixed on the other's lips, while their hands caressed the other's body with a slowness which became tormenting. Entwined, they shuffled towards the bedroom, George managing to switch off that evil air-conditioner on the way. Above the vast bed hung two paintings of pineapples and straw hats and black women with pointed breasts to remind the occupants that they were in the Caribbean.

Gavin pushed George down on to the bed, but restrained himself heroically from throwing himself on top of her. He sat beside her, like a musician preparing to play an instrument. How she loved him when he was about to make love like this, something like pain clouding the intensity of his gaze. She waited. Not long now. They were coming into their own kingdom, safe from real life. He leaned over her and, without touching her with his hands, began to kiss her lips. Their tongues made love. Then one of his hands encircled her breast while the other sought between her legs with a gentleness more violent in its effect than violence. They couldn't hold out much longer like this, joined only by their lips, his fingers on those lower lips, her hands on his cock. When they could bear it no longer, he laid his full length on her, parting her legs with his and, like the prow of a boat moving into harbour, pressed into her with infinite delicate slowness. ('A centimetre a second,' she would tell the inquiring Ellen, who'd note: 'Quarter of a knot an hour. For a sailor, you must admit.')

When it arrived, their orgasm was almost waveless, so intense was everything that led up to and succeeded it. And it seemed to go on for ever, perhaps even twice. Who could say? Certainly not these two, lying motionless to prolong the peak of joy.

'I'm glad I was able to hold out this time,' whispered Gavin, just before they fell asleep to the sound of a sudden heavy shower freshening the night air.

Next morning their eyes were bluer, bodies more free. George grew more beautiful by the minute, anointed by Gavin's unwavering desire. She felt like Alice in Wonderland, where the laws of the world above held no sway. But for Gavin it was the same old story. All this went against everything he believed in. For the moment he decided not to fight it. They still had nine days to satisfy their mutual obsession. They gazed at each other with incredulous gratitude.

Yet again, though, George wondered why they could

never get further than the simplest love-making. 'Poor things, you're still at the ABC stage of fucking,' Ellen would have said if she could have seen them. But they had never been together long enough to elaborate their technique. Each time they started from scratch, and by the time they were sure enough to try anything a little more subtle, it was time to part again. So George suffered from sexual bulimia when with Gavin, ravenous for even the most basic caresses, hungering for the country bread and carafe wine of love. Nouvelle cuisine could come later. She wondered if this was what her father meant by nymphomania, a word he always uttered with distaste, though she thought it was beautiful. She felt like a nymph, but Gavin was the nymph-maniac. Maniac but innocent in exploring the joy of intimacy, tentative, as if afraid of inventing some perversion.

'You know something, *Karedig*?' he said hesitantly one evening. 'It may seem funny, but ever since you taught me to stay with you after we've made love, I like our smell.'

George tried not to smile. She felt a tender pride, like a mother bird encouraging her chick to fly. (Go on, little cormorant. Don't be scared. Yes, that's the way. Off you go.)

After the second day they escaped from the main beach patrolled by hot-dog and Coke vendors and poisoned by the music which blared out of the bar from noon onwards, and set off to find an unspoiled corner. They found it at the tip of the island, a place called Negrim. There the stretch of sand was free, and no one made them rent a deck chair or a sun umbrella. In a palm hut under the mangroves which shaded the beach, they enjoyed the local soup the grand restaurants never deigned to serve.

They ate at home in the evenings, then went dancing in

the open air, a reminder of that first dance at Ty Chupenn Gwen where it all began. And every night, when they got back, they agreed not to make love, because they'd made love in the late afternoon, and would make love again in the middle of the night. But of course they ended up making love. And those were the best times of all. How marvellously predictable their responses were!

In the morning George stayed in bed while Gavin got their breakfast of cornflakes, and eggs and bacon. Then they would join one of the excursions like 'Village Life' or 'The Wild River Tour'. Their group would include talkative Americans, who delighted Gavin by calling George 'your wife', Canadians who would be drunk before noon on beer and Germans sporting shorts and cameras and hanging on the tour guide's every word.

The odd thing was, though they'd spent so few days together in their lives, they felt as intimate as an old couple. For instance, George had never before been able to talk about her periods with any man, to say how she always felt sexier just before them. She had been brought up to silence about such matters, and to conceal every shred of evidence, each month, from the men in her life. But Gavin didn't seem to feel the least distaste for female functions, perhaps because he loved her so unconditionally or because he lived close to the elements. He wanted to know everything about her, and she found herself telling him things she would never have dreamed of saying to anyone else. You could go a lifetime and never find a man who gave you this sense of serene shamelessness, but Gavin even made it possible for her to let him see her blood, so sure was she of his tenderness for all of her, for each hair, each grimace, each gesture, each flaw. He was one of those rare men who are loving after sex, as if he still wanted her enough to touch and kiss and stroke and whisper. It was an unbearable pleasure sometimes.

'Lozerech, tell me something. I've been thinking about it a lot. Is it just because of this,' George fingered the half-curled anchovy fillet resting on Gavin's thigh, 'that we make such elaborate arrangements, go through so many hoops, to be together? Are we just animals, giving in to our instincts, to our skin, in the end?'

'I'd say it's more than that, myself. Something deeper . . .'

'But suppose the deepest thing we have is just that, our skin? At least our bodies know exactly what they want. *They* don't listen to reason, they're implacable. You're not keen on the idea? You'd like it better if it was something to do with our souls?'

Gavin ran his hand through his mop of hair to clarify his thoughts. He always did that when he was thinking.

'I just don't like being in the power of something I don't understand, that's all.'

'Do you think you understand faith, then? Or love, when it makes you do crazy things?'

'No, I don't understand any of it. I just know that when I'm with you everything's all right, and I don't have to bother myself with questions. But when I'm by myself, yes, it does worry me. I don't like feeling that I'm not the skipper.'

'It's completely different for me. With you I feel I'm learning something vital, that we have something strong, a mystic union. It's as if we were accepting a decree of nature. Not many people hear nature's decrees.'

Gavin listened, troubled and distrustful. George was getting him all tangled up in fine words. What good would they be to him when he tossed and turned in his bunk, worrying whether he was weak-minded or a shit or both for not being able to end this affair which, sad to admit, gave life its savour.

'George, you'll write our story one day, won't you?' he asked some time later. She was flabbergasted. They were lounging by the Club swimming pool. A glaringly blue pool surrounded by brown and orange umbrellas advertising Pepsi-Cola. You have to make the most of all this ugliness, to drain it to the dregs, she'd been thinking, for it's an art doing things you detest, from time to time.

Gavin looked handsome and American that evening, in seersucker trousers and a pink polo neck – not a colour he would normally have dreamed of wearing but which she had forced him to accept as a gift. He was so relaxed too, replete with their endless love-making. And the way he said, 'Georch' with his Breton lisp put her at his mercy!

'You will, won't you?'

'But what on earth do you want me to write? They went to bed, they got up, they went to bed again, they fucked and fucked and fucked and he made her feel wonderful and she made them shine, those fish eyes of his . . .'

'Well, what eyes do you expect a fisherman to have?'

'Your eyes aren't anything like a fish's, really.'

'Tuna have beautiful eyes you know. Black with silver rings round. When they're alive in the sea, that is. You've never seen a live one, you wouldn't know.'

'True enough. But I do know you have eyes which are totally depraved in the sea or out. At least they are when you're with me. It's all I can do to stop myself from yelling out loud, "Yes – whenever you want, wherever you want, however you want!" I worry people might notice. It must be written all over me.'

'Well, write that too. Sometimes I don't know why you keep on loving me. It needs explaining how it can happen, a story like ours. You'll know how to do it.'

'But I wouldn't know. It's the hardest thing in the world to write a love story. Anyway, I'm not a novelist.'

'You write history. Can't be much different. I don't know why, but I'd really like to see it all written down in a book, everything we've had, so I could be sure it's true, that it really happened to me. Maybe it's because I've never been able to say a word about it to a single soul.'

'You're right. It's such a relief to be able to talk about it. I can talk to Frédérique, and to François. I've told you about him and Luce, remember? And Sidney at least knows that you exist.'

'I'd be in dead trouble myself if my wife found out,' said Gavin, suddenly despondent. 'When I'm with you, I'm a completely different person, as if I was in someone else's clothes. Then, when I put on those sandals you're so rude about, it's as if I've gone back to being my real self. But there it is. If anyone had told me I'd be able to carry on like this I'd have laughed in their face for sure.'

'Let's have another drink,' said George quickly. His eyes were filling, and he would be mortified by crying, she knew. Tears were to be resisted.

'You see, right now, I'd sooner die than never see you again. But as soon as we're away from each other I tell myself I'm mad, and it can't go on like this.'

They were silent. George ran her hand over those great wrists of his which filled her with such tenderness. Contact with the little hairs sent a current of excitement through her. Then, so quietly that she could scarcely hear him, Gavin said, 'I want you so much that it'll never end, will it?'

Neither of them spoke for a moment, luxuriating in the twilight and their provisional liberty. Words had no power to hurt them yet, while the night lay before them, and more nights and days to come, an ocean of love waiting for them to sail it.

'Shall I tell you how it could best be ended between us?' asked George.

Gavin raised an eyebrow, bewildered.

'I'll tell you how. It would be for us to live together properly. I'd drive you mad, and you'd fly into those rages of yours . . .'

'That's what you're always saying,' he answered, stung. 'Me, I'm dead sure I could love you my whole life long. If I wasn't, I'd've sent you packing long ago.' He didn't smile at those last words. 'I'm not happy, you know. It doesn't seem right, cheating on Marie-Josée, and I can't get used to it. But I can't do anything about it. If I could've I'd get a divorce.'

George smiled lovingly. Now his grammar seemed touching, though she had often cringed when he talked about the 'doc', or when he called the sea 'the drink'. He couldn't see what was wrong with 'doc' or 'the drink'. The fact that she could not make him see it was the very drama of social class and prejudice and culture.

'Anyway, it's you who wouldn't be able to put up with me,' he went on, very softly. 'I know damn well I'm not at your level. But funny though it seems, it doesn't matter to me. I like it when you correct the way I speak. It's your job, after all. Look how you've taught me to travel, to look out for things I'd not have noticed otherwise. People like me, we don't have time for looking. We don't even know we're living.'

'True enough, Lozerech, my lad. And while we're on the subject of living, do you realise we've gone at least five hours without making love? You're not ill or anything?'

Gavin burst out laughing the over-loud laugh of a man who lives among men. Laughter was the only antidote against the certainty that they would never be able to live together, that and a touch of coarseness. Gavin loved it when George was coarse occasionally. It made her more human, more approachable. Sometimes she seemed so foreign to him.

'Right then, want to come and do a spot of – living, do you?' He looked at her teasingly, confident of her answer.

'You filthy beast. It's always youah tempting me. Youah, youah,' she responded, mocking his broad Breton.

'Laugh at me, would youah? And how do youah say "youah" anyway? I thought I'd lost my accent, being away so long.'

'You could never lose it. You can't even hear yourself. And all the men you work with have the same one. I'm mad about your accent. Who knows if it's not one of the main reasons for my shameless attraction to you.'

Arms around each other, they made for cell number 1718. The beach was deserted, with only the pelicans squawking and quarrelling. At night the birds imagined they were still on their own territory and forgot there was the Hilton and the Holiday Inn and all the other tourist nests. Suddenly, at the thought of the winter she would return to in a few days, George had an impulse to run across the sand once more. As usual Gavin sat on the sea wall, waiting for her. It never occurred to him to do anything athletic, and people who did made him laugh. She raced across the firm sand, splashing now and then in the tumbling water which traced garlands of foam on the beach, ebbing and flowing like the breathing of the sea. The mysterious rhythm of the moving waves was like the rhythm of love. (*'Can't you ever think about anything else?'* 'You've got it wrong again. There are privileged moments when everything is love.') As she ran, free and light, George fused with everything around her, assimilating it with her entire being, enjoying the easy movements of her body and the dull beat of her heels on the sand. She felt born anew, as if recalling some fleeting distant memory of those first creatures who left the sea to breathe the strange element, air. Her desire, her love, formed only one of the strands of the spell which held her. She wished she could hoard all this happiness for ever. But love can't be stockpiled any more than you can harvest sunlight. Each experience is unique and vanishes like waves which recede then melt into the ocean.

Gavin was waiting for her on the harbour wall, swinging his legs. He couldn't see the point of an ocean without boats, and holidaying bored him. His pastime, his reason for being here, was George.

'You're all wet, like a mermaid,' he said, folding her in his arms. 'Do you want me to brush the sand off your feet. I've got the towel.'

'No, don't. I love the feel of sand. It proves to me I'm not in Paris, you see.'

Funny notions these Paris people had. He held her closer. The only time she didn't feel foreign to him was when they were making love.

They adored the hour just before sleep. Gavin was always in bed first, watching George as she pottered about getting ready for bed, creaming a patch of sunburnt skin, checking that she'd washed the sand from every cranny.

'When you've quite done . . .' he would soon say in exasperation.

She flung herself on him, and it was as if someone had thrown a switch. Current flooded through them, everything shone and crackled. She had read of similar phenomena in novels and dismissed them as preposterous. But this shock was indisputable. The only thing that made her hold back at all was the fear of Gavin dropping dead from his exertions. And the state of her own private parts. She was astounded that Gavin still found her body so stirring, that he could still be enthralled by that slice of water melon he already knew by heart, that he could still shake when he touched her mound or felt her labia, and go white as his fingers came down into her valley. How could this man, who went into ecstasy over her cunt, not be at all interested in Picasso? How could he travel three thousand miles to lie on top of her and not bother to go round the corner to see Notre-Dame? ('He likes my cunt better, that's all,' she told her chaperone defiantly. '*Oh, to be loved to the very depths of one's being . . .*' the chaperone spat back.)

'Darling Lozerech, tell me what it is down there that gives you so much pleasure. Tell me what other women's are like. Tell me how I'm different.'

And he told her that what she had between her legs was a magic garden, a veritable Disney World, a Luna Park, with rollercoasters, a water chute and a bearded lady. He said that he found new corners to negotiate every time, new places to park. That she was the owner of amazing expanding walls, of secret moving parts, of spaces which breathed in mysterious rhythms. In short, that she drove him wild. In short, what every woman dreams of hearing. George even began to believe that his non-stop erections were a tribute to her charms, though she knew, really, that they were only due to his exceptional potency. But he told George that it was all due to her magic garden, even though she had only the vaguest idea of how things worked down there. She had never bothered to follow Ellen's advice on 'having autonomy over your own vagina'. Ellen was insistent on exercise. 'Start with twenty or thirty contractions of your pelvic floor every morning. Do them whenever you're at the hairdresser or waiting for a bus, for example. After a bit you'll be able to do two or three hundred contractions a day, and no one ever notices that you're doing them. To make sure that your vagina has reached Olympic fitness, practise stopping the flow two or three times when you pass water.' At the thought of an Olympic-class vagina, George couldn't resist trying.

She told Gavin who laughed. It was beyond him that anyone could seriously write a book about such things. It just confirmed his opinion that all brainy people were off their trolleys.

'*You* don't need any of that,' he said with touching faith. Oh, don't I? thought George. How nice that he has no suspicion about feminine wiles.

At other times, he would get anxious, torn by his morality. 'It's not normal like, is it, me getting more and more pleasure from your pleasure, and your excitement being almost as exciting as mine?'

'So you think it's abnormal to want to give someone pleasure?'

Their teeth clashed in a kiss. Gavin drew back.

'You're such an animal. If you go on like this I'll get another chipped tooth.'

'Fine. Fine. I'll stop. Anyway, I've got cramp in that pelvic floor of mine. Lack of exercise, I expect.'

She picked up a book and he fell into one of his brief, stubborn sleeps, like a cross child, or a seaman, ready to wake at the slightest noise. He would be alert in a second, not just open-eyed but bolt upright, shouting, 'What's going on?' George would soothe him as she soothed Loïc after a night-mare. 'It's all right, darling. Go back to sleep. It's nothing.' And he would say, 'Not nothing. You're here. That's really something!'

Those nights, in the small hours when defences are down, he would start talking about himself. She listened to this sudden eloquence in him, this man who'd been the little boy of her childhood, the love of her adolescence, and now the captain, taciturn and brave. He told her of the high points of his life at sea, things only a fisherman can know. The funny times too, like last summer, when for the first time the crew went home for their annual leave by air. Most of them had never flown before.

'You should have seen them, and that great jet. Total panic. They were more scared in that machine than they ever were on their trawler even in the biggest storm. Result? By the time we touched ground every man jack of them was pissed out of his mind. Hey, you're not listening. I'm boring you.'

'No, no, I've heard every word. Pissed out of their minds you said.'

'I don't know why I'm telling you all this. Hey, that reminds me. Have I ever told you about that time we . . . ?'

As he spoke he stroked her so her body idled along paths of pleasure. They put out the light to feel closer. Now they were on watch, the two of them, on the bridge of a boat cutting its way through the night, towards the end of the world.

★

There's no way of avoiding Disney World in Florida. All the Americans they'd met were clear about that, and the ones who'd been there were full of enthusiasm. For once, there was something that Gavin actually wanted to see, the only famous place in the United States he'd heard of. And since they had to change planes in Miami, they decided to leave Jamaica early so as not to return to Europe without having visited the great swamps of the Everglades, the museums, not to mention the famous cloisters from St Bernard's monastery in Segovia, built in 1141 and 'brought to the US of A stone by stone, by Randolph Hearst' as the travel agent informed them in an awed voice, as though this dismantling had added inestimable value to the masterpiece.

That same tour operator insisted that they must spend at least thirty-six hours in Walt Disney's Magic Kingdom, and made all the arrangements with suspicious zeal. It was only at Miami airport, when they were settled into a limousine the size of a Paris studio flat that George started to panic. Its air-conditioning and tinted windows were designed to imprison one in a vacuum, cut off from fresh air, blue sky, natural smells, and since Gavin didn't speak a word of English, it was she who had to guide this sealed capsule through a nightmare world. There did not seem to be a single human being by the roadside, to direct one through the network of vast suspension bridges, colossal road interchanges conceived by madmen, motorways with eight lanes, along which purred thousands of indistinguishable cars at indistinguishable speeds. They didn't seem to be going anywhere, apparently content to bowl along at fifty miles an hour as proof of their existence. Why would anyone want to go anywhere? The towns were identical, whether they be named Tampa, Clearwater, Bonita Springs, Naples, or Vanderbilt Beach.

Crushed by these surreal surroundings, George decided that someone must be mad. Perhaps it was Europeans, villagers living in funny communities clustered around the church, with their little grocery-cafés, the local drunk prostrate on the pavement, the smell of bread wafting from the bakery and the ironmonger in his grey overall. Or perhaps it was the mutants here, swarming endlessly along the monstrous network of roads like a giant train set, flanked by a thousand shopping malls the size of the Taj Mahal, with their marble fountains, conservatories and cinemas all showing the same films. These were succeeded by residential areas which looked as if they had been completed only that day, so tidy and bare were they and their unnaturally smooth lawns. Then they passed through city centres made up of thirty-storey mausoleums inhabited by thousands of 'senior citizens' awaiting death in luxury, and of detached houses whose principal adornment was the paved driveway leading to the triple garage with its door straight into the house so the householders could get in and out of their cars without ever setting foot in the garden. Not that these spaces deserved the name of garden: there wasn't a flower to be seen, not a deck chair, not one overturned child's bicycle, just green space, watered twice a day by an invisible sprinkler, even when it was raining, because it had been programmed for the season. Every now and again there was a touching patch of waste ground between two skyscrapers, its brambles and thistles reminding one that there was such a thing as nature, that grass doesn't grow ready-mown.

But Florida never allows you to forget that it is, first and foremost, an amusement park. Every three or four miles hortatory billboards directed drivers to slow down so as not to miss the most intelligent seals, the fiercest tigers, the most

Indian Indians in the world. Sure enough it wasn't long before a Spanish-style gateway loomed. It could have been an Aztec temple or a gothic fortress but in fact it was where one purchased tickets for Nature – for the Jungle Gardens, the Wild Animal Park, the Alligator Farm. These oxymorons, emblazoned in neon (how could a jungle be a garden, a park contain wild beasts, an alligator be a farm animal?), were, thought George, more than enough to make a reasonable creature bolt for it. Starting with the tiger. Was it only a hundred and fifty years since Spain had yielded this great marshy peninsula to the United States? George tried to explain to Gavin why it all dismayed her so, but Lozerech was too smitten by the opulence of the 'Sunshine State'.

They stopped to visit the humble home of Mr Henry Flagler, who had been one of the founders of Standard Oil, a fact that provoked such reverence you'd have thought he had written the *Divine Comedy*. 'The Flagler Museum has been preserved in its original state since the year nineteen-oh-six,' the guide informed them in a tone of deep respect, as if describing a rare, ancient vintage. The drawing room had been extracted from the Palazzo Dogale at Mantua, the ceiling torn from a house on the Giudecca at Venice, there were Pre-Raphaelite walls and Pompeiian bathrooms. The mosaics were authentic, the oil paintings genuine, but had lost their souls on the journey, and now smacked of fakery.

'Just listen to that guide,' George began, then stopped herself. There was no point in trying to make Gavin understand. He had never been to Venice or Mantua or Pompeii, so why should he share her outrage? He had always thought that antiques had to be dusty and chipped, just because they were antiques. He was amazed by the way everything here looked good as new, glossy and gilded, every sculpture intact, no toes or noses missing. Old things could be terrific, after all!

It was a terrible mistake to go to museums with Lozerech, George decided. All he was good for was love. They should have stayed near a bed.

Off they went again. George had learned that there were only two or three museums worthy of note, but they were separated by miles and miles of featureless road. With Sidney she would have been able to make fun of it all. His devastating wit would simply have banished Florida from the map of the civilised world. But Gavin noticed nothing: for him a landscape was simply a landscape.

But he tried to keep George amused while she drove.

'Listen, this is a good one. Do you know why beer goes in and comes out the other end so quickly?'

No, George certainly did not know why.

'Because it doesn't need to change colour on the way.' He pealed with laughter, watching her reaction.

She didn't even attempt to smile. Once and for all, she wanted him to know that what might go down well with the boozers of Brittany had not the slightest interest for her. But she knew he would just think she had no sense of humour. One day she might try to explain to him what humour was. No, what good would it do? It's always the people without one who are touchiest on the subject of a sense of humour. Gavin changed the subject.

'Hey, look. They're building a new house there.'

'People don't usually build old houses,' blurted George.

'Right,' said Gavin coldly, and retreated into silence.

Hunger came to their rescue. Seduced by frequent signs promising Real Fresh Seafood (what was fake fresh seafood, wondered George) they stopped at a Fisherman's Lodge – or, perhaps, a Pirates' Grotto or a Sailor's Cove. The last real fresh fisherman had been forced to hang up his nets long ago, and the 'grottoes' had twenty-storey apartment buildings on top of them. Gavin and George didn't see one single fishing port the whole time they were there, not one real fishmonger selling identifiable fish with heads and tails and fins. All they saw were pallid fillets sealed in plastic in supermarket freezers.

They ate oily tasteless oysters, detached from their shells and sedulously rinsed of any flavour of the sea, and clams so plump that it felt obscene to bite into them. After lunch, they swam from an anonymous stretch of the endless beach which runs for hundreds of miles along Florida's east coast, dotted everywhere with old men and women in deck chairs and lollipop-coloured clothes. Then drove off again, fast, because George wanted to see the famous Cloisters, dissected in Spain and reconstituted here on a patch of land between two high-rises. This 'real' monastery bore as much relation to a Cistercian abbey as a robot to a human being. Henceforth George treated the word 'real' with profound scepticism. The stones might be Spanish but the tiles were Mexican, while the floor of the chapel was covered with household slate.

'There really were monks here, then?' asked Gavin. They were strolling round the cloister which, inexplicably, still retained some sense of the spiritual.

'How could there have been?' asked George crossly. 'The whole thing's a fake. It's only here on a whim of Randolph Hearst. Have you seen *Citizen Kane*?'

'N-no. Doesn't mean anything to me.'

'It's an Orson Welles film about Hearst's life. He was a multimillionaire, a newspaper tycoon, and he . . . I'll explain it all later.'

George sighed at the thought of all the explaining she'd have to do, starting with the *Mayflower*, going on to the Conquistadores, the genocide of the native Americans, every event requiring its preparation and its sequel. It would take ten years of schooling to instil in him the elements of history, geography, literature. What a desert Lozerech's life sometimes seemed. How could he possibly understand a country when all he saw was what was presented?

By the evening George was in a foul temper. She resented herself for resenting him. To make matters worse, their money was running out, and they had to eat in a place serving the very worst of fast food. Then they booked into the deceptively named Sea View Motel, whose brochure was full of craftily angled shots to disguise the fact that only two of its windows overlooked the sea. Their room opened on to the car park. Or, rather, didn't open. The windows were hermetically sealed. And they were next to the ice machine which crushed and crunched all night in the corridor outside. To that was added the din of the air-conditioning and the bulldozer which rumbled up and down the beach all evening raking the sand. They had twin beds separated by an immovable bedside table. In Florida, evidently, people didn't sleep together. Nor make love in the daytime. No bidet. Unless they took a shower before and after. Or washed at the basin. Didn't Americans know how unattractive a woman looked when she was washing herself down there, knees bent, legs spread? As is customary in the States, the WC was right next to the bath, allowing the lucky person taking a bath to savour every whiff. George gave up trying to understand the rationale behind the layout of sanitary facilities in the New World.

'Even us Bretons do better than that,' remarked Gavin. 'At least we have them at the bottom of the garden. Maybe

Americans do it straight into plastic bags, the way they wrap their fish. Look, even the glasses are wrapped in plastic.'

Lavatory humour is one of the best ways of regressing to childhood and George allowed herself to laugh, to forgive Gavin his lack of culture for this one night. She even let him make love to her. In a spirit of penitence, to make up for her evil-mindedness, she even took him into her mouth, and swallowed a mouthful of him.

Not great. She couldn't be truly in love, she accused herself, not if she didn't love his taste. She restrained herself from rushing to rinse her mouth out. ('*It's never the taste of sperm that women like,*' the chaperone assured her. '*What they like is the taste of male pleasure. There's a difference!*') And dried semen felt so nasty. George could put up with it on her thighs, but not when it stiffened on her chin. Perhaps women jibbed at swallowing millions of potential babies. She herself didn't feel she had the soul of an ogress. Indeed, that night, she didn't feel she had a soul at all.

The night was short anyway since they were on the road by six, all prepared for Tour Number Four: two days at Disney World surrounded by battalions of families. You'd think a new Tower of Babel had fallen, so many different countries were represented. There were hordes of children, most of whom were already dressed as Mickey Mouse or Donald Duck. Perched on the benches of a 'real' fake mini-ature steam-train, their group ('Be sure to wear your badges on your lapels, folks!') chugged within sight of a neo-Gothic medieval castle in pink and white, its turrets and crenellations commanding Main Street, lined with buildings fake through and through, except for the shops which sold real crap for real dollars.

Tour Number Four meant that they had passes for every

single attraction in the Magic Kingdom. There was the inter-planetary trip in an authentic rocket with acceleration effects and an optical illusion of the receding earth – three and a half minutes. And the landing on Mars – two minutes. Twenty Thousand Leagues under the Sea – six and a quarter minutes, all of them spent surrounded by sea monsters which even the most short-sighted could spot as phony at ten yards. And the *pièce de résistance* of culture and patriotism: the Hall of Presidents, in which animatronics made life-sized robots move, and trivial sayings flicker across a giant screen. A Lincoln moulded in wax gave an edifying homily. There was nothing to remind you that he had been assassinated for that might upset the children. The grand finale was a display of fifty presidents in front of the star-spangled banner, inspiring everyone to behave themselves in the wonderful country which had invented liberty.

George found herself condemning everything from the moment they arrived. Nothing found favour in her eyes, least of all Gavin's bedazzlement. His eyes were round with amazement wherever they went, his mouth hanging open. Like all the other little boys from everywhere, thought George, united by such excitement as to forget even to stuff themselves with popcorn or their garish ices which melted in poisonous colours down their windcheaters. But once on this production line there was no way of escaping. The vis-itors, organised into groups of a hundred, were channelled, timed, stimulated to an immutable programme, herded politely but firmly along the one-way passages from which there was no way out. An omnipresent voice, a sort of Big Brother – whose words of advice were in fact orders – directed them to rest areas at distances designed for the aver-age walker, rest rooms for the average bladder, and candy stores positioned so that the most myopic child could spot them. Moms and dads were held to ransom by offspring pointing sticky fingers at other people's offspring who had already attained the sugary paradise and were covered in chocolate and stained with chemical drinks.

There was no avoiding the Haunted House or the Caribbean Pirates' Den, both of them hallucinating in their mock 'historical' approach. Here were pillaged towns teeming with drunken robots who threatened the spectators with their blowpipes and sang bawdy songs which had been carefully censored. There were dungeons crammed with treasure, shipwrecked sailors hanging lividly from cardboard rocks, skeletons with careful tatters of uniform clinging to their bones, alligators automatically snapping plastic jaws as the wagons went by. A miracle of technology at the service of the most rudimentary emotions. And it had to be a new emotion every second. So people were propelled from one scene to the next, each scene meticulous and so detailed that there wasn't time to stop, much less to think.

What exasperated her most was that George seemed to be the only person to find it all depressing. The moms and dads were thrilled, would leave convinced that they had learned everything there was to know about Polynesian life, the Amazonian jungle, space travel. They would imagine they had, with their own eyes, seen the true descendants of the native Caribs, with no one to tell them that the last surviving Caribs, trapped on their last island, had thrown themselves off a cliff rather than fall into the hands of our glorious Western civilisation.

'Just look at them,' she let fly. 'They're just so damn proud of it all! They're so proud of Disney World you'd think they'd built Chartres cathedral with their own hands.'

'What's wrong with that? Why should it bother you that other people are having a good time? You think that anyone who doesn't like what you like is a moron,' said Gavin dejected as if he had at last seen the gulf that divided them. 'I think it's all terrific. I've never seen anything like it. It makes me happy like a kid who's never seen anything but the circus we had every summer on the shore back in Finistère.'

George managed not to say: yes, you've never seen anything, that's the problem, and what's worse, you've never looked. She resented him for Disney World as a whole, all those beatific faces and wide eyes. And there was still another day of it tomorrow. What now awaited them was one of the twelve hundred bedrooms of the Contemporary World Resort. Gavin would love it: it had a little monorail which sped through the reception areas every eight minutes with a freight of infantile families taking their pleasures as seriously as their work.

'I'll have to beg off tomorrow,' she told him. 'I can't face another day of Mr Disney's Magic World. If I see one more Mickey Mouse I'll throw up. You'll find World Circus and Marineland much more fun without me. I bet even the whales have got Mickey Mouse ears.'

For the first time Gavin saw how unpleasant George could be. Crestfallen, he tried to reason with her but reason was a territory into which he would do better not to venture with her.

'You're quick to sit in judgement on people who aren't the same as you,' he said. And added sententiously, 'It takes all sorts to make a world.'

'Is that so?'

Gavin bit his lip. This stubborn, plebeian expression must be the one he wore when he was being ticked off by a gaffer and didn't dare answer back. He agreed to go alone the next day.

'Anyway I've paid for the ticket.'

'It would be a pity to waste it,' concurred George.

He wondered whether she was being nasty or really agreeing. Their attitudes to money were so different that he never knew when she was just teasing. That was part of the problem.

Both of them felt grubby and worn-out, and on one point they agreed: Disney World was exhausting.

'Shall I run you a nice hot bath?' Gavin sweetly offered when they got to their room. George couldn't help herself.

'No, I'd prefer a nasty cold one.'

'Christ, why are you so awful sometimes.'

'Because you come out with such clichés. It really gets on my nerves.'

'It's me altogether who gets on your nerves. If you think I hadn't noticed . . .'

'Look, we take it in turns to get on each other's nerves. It can't be helped. It's been such an exhausting day, I'm shattered.'

She didn't tell him that she had found a hard, painful swelling on her vulva which she was frightened might develop into an abscess. ('*Come on, it's only an inflamed Bartholin gland,*' interrupted the chaperone, now convinced that she'd studied medicine. '*All that trafficking down there, no wonder it's swollen. All very nice these sexual goings-on of yours, but you're going to have to calm down a bit, my girl. And have you seen your mouth? Sins are always punished at their source!*')

It was true. George had a cold sore on her top lip. Disney strikes again! She was going to look like Donald Duck for their last day together. The idea made her behave even worse.

Hurt, Gavin withdrew into that formidable shell of his. For the first time since they had known each other they wondered what they were doing together. Both longed to be with their own kind, their tribe, people who thought as they did, liked the same sort of things.

When they went to bed that evening George took a book from her case while Gavin opened a thriller which he had bought at the airport. He blew at the pages to separate them, and licked his finger every time he turned over. That got on her nerves too, watching him laboriously spell out each word, his eyes moving from left to right along the line of print as if he were deciphering an elaborate code. He was yawning before he had got through three pages, but he didn't want to go to sleep before George.

Once the light was out he moved cautiously towards, her, ready to retreat at the first sign of rejection.

'I just want to put my arms round you. Can I . . .'

She snuggled her back into his belly as a sign of acquiescence. The moment she was locked into the security belt of Gavin's arms she felt a sense of peace. There was no cheating: he didn't move a finger. He had even tucked his offending member between his thighs, happy just hugging her. What an idiot! Didn't he know by now that the slightest contact of their bodies was enough to trigger them off? George turned suddenly to him, and desire took over instantly, sweeping them both along that vital course on which they never disappointed each other.

There were just the Everglades to see. At least no one had yet succeeded in concreting over these vast swampy tracts and acres of shifting mud to which only mangroves were able to cling.

Here, more than anywhere else in America, it was possible to drive hundreds of miles without seeing any alteration in the landscape. The entire length of that interminable straight line which joins the Atlantic coast to the Gulf of Mexico was a melancholy world of swamps bordered with stunted trees. Apart from the trucks and the huge, noiseless limousines, the only living creatures were birds: egrets, crested cranes, herons, buzzards, eagles, and the state emblem, pelicans, neither wild nor tame but so weary from their migration that they just perched on the posts of the piers where tourists embarked for their boat trips. The birds' only distraction was having their photographs taken six hundred times a day.

Because of its seductive name they went to Everglades City for lunch. It turned out to be a sort of urban agglomeration, neither city nor village, at the end of the peninsula. In a Swiss chalet (well, why not? there was no local style) the menu offered the best Fresh Seafood in Florida. Fresh it certainly wasn't. As for the sea, according to their *Guide Bleu*, it was the most polluted stretch in the world. That left food. But it was a cheerful welcoming place, and the Americans around them were happily tucking into their disgusting mountains of food crowned with tomato ketchup and served on paper plates. To George and Gavin the clams, the cod steaks, were indistinguishable in texture, but then everyone knows what grumblers the French are.

'Feels like chewing on minced plastic Disney animals. Don't you think?'

Gavin nodded, still wary.

'Have you seen the Kofaymat?' he asked.

'Kofaymat? Oh, you mean Coffeemate . . .'

'You know I've got a Breton accent, whatever language I'm speaking.'

'At least they're honest enough not to call it milk. Look, it says "Non-dairy product".'

'Yet I bet they're just like us in Europe, with mountains of dried milk.'

'Have you *seen* the list of ingredients? Listen. Partially hydrogenated coconut oil, sodium casinate, monoglycerides, diglycerides, phosphates, sodium, and of course artificial colouring and artificial flavouring. Whatever sort of artificial colouring do you need to make something white?'

'It doesn't taste too bad, though,' said Gavin.

'Mmm . . . especially the diglyceride. It's exquisite. Shame it does nothing to hide the taste of the coffee.'

'And have you noticed the butter? It looks just like shaving cream.'

The cheese at least was Austrian gruyère, and the wine was Italian. It seemed to them suddenly that their little Europe was a treasure store of dairy cows, of multitudinous cheeses, wines, fish, of churches built over hundreds of years standing in the places they were built for; little Europe, brimming with castles and beautiful things, with rivers, each different from the others, with styles of cooking and architecture which changed from region to fiercely independent region – Basque, Breton, Tyrolean. They were delighted to be Europeans, then French, and, above all, Breton, delighted to be with each other once more.

They still had several hours for the swamps and mangroves, the egrets, herons, cranes, buzzards and pelicans, not to mention two or three Seminole villages, erected beside the turnpike so that tourists didn't have to tire themselves discovering the Indian way of life in an authentic setting. This setting consisted of three huts, one of which was a souvenir shop selling embroidered leather belts and clumsily stitched moccasins. They wouldn't have qualified as authentic had the Indians learned to sew. There was also a bamboo hedge not quite concealing a modern trailer complete with television aerial. This was where the Indians lived when they weren't acting out the Seminole Way of Life.

Gavin was determined to spend some of his skipper's booty on their last night, and booked a table at a luxury restaurant which was said to have good food. But the Curse of Disney pursued them still, though this time not with a mob of children, but of old people. Gavin and George were the only ones who didn't need a walking frame or crutches, the only ones without tremors of the hands or chin, the only ones with authentically imperfect teeth. All the other diners displayed even rows of impeccable dentures. George imagined those shrivelled willies inside the $500 slacks, all those forlorn, abandoned vulvas. She felt pity for the knotted hands, the wrinkled necks, the scabs between the colourless strands of hair on the men's bald scalps, and the brown marks on the faces of the faded blondes. Suddenly Gavin's arrogant strength seemed to her the only lifebuoy in this sea of lost souls, and what he concealed in his $70 trousers the only antidote to death.

The cabaret was a line of undulating 'native' dancers whose gleaming insolent black skins seemed immune from the ravages of time, and whose supple grace must have been heart-breaking for old people whose movements got stiffer by the day.

'There's one thing you have to give the blacks,' said Gavin (Oh God, please don't let him say it!) 'and that's their sense of rhythm. It's in the blood.' (Snickers from the chaperone, who hadn't uttered a peep since before Disney World: *'There you are. Twelve days and you've already had enough. The cunt's*

156

no foundation for a real relationship.' 'Shut up you wizened old virgin. You've never known how special it can be.' *'My dear girl! Someone only has to tickle you in the right places and your vagina gets turned on and you start singing the* Magnificat. *It's nothing but a light secretion of the glands, a simple stimulation of the pleasure points.')*

For the moment they indulged in the simple stimulation of their salivary glands. But not even the superb Oysters Rockefeller could prevent Gavin from worrying about old age in his turn.

'Just think, it's only a few years and I'll be retired. As soon as I've made up my full pension I'll stop working. We'd have enough to live on then, even if we didn't have as much as this lot.'

'But how will you bear staying at home the whole year round? I just can't imagine you without your ship.'

'As far as staying at home goes, I've never done it, it's true. Still, I'd get a little fishing boat and go out just for the hell of it. I'm not one to stay put looking after the vegetable patch.'

For most fishermen gardening, working the land, means being bored to death. They might know exactly where they are in the ocean, just by the colour of the water, but can't tell a peony from an anemone in a garden.

'But before that I've got a scheme,' he went on, cutting his T-bone steak into small pieces on his plate. 'I must tell you about it. Mad idea, though.'

'What sort of mad idea? You're not going to give up fishing?'

'You must be joking. There's my pension for a start. I'm not entitled to enough yet . . . Anyway, being stuck on land before I have to, it'd make me sick. No, it's something my cousin from Douarnenez – you know the one, Marcel Le Louarn – talked about. Could be a lot of money in it. And what with Joël never being able to work, we're going to need money.'

He hesitated before going on. He kept his eyes lowered, not looking at George, crumbling his bread on the tablecloth.

'Trouble is, it could be a bit tricky for you and me. I'd be somewhere off South Africa.'

'What do you mean, tricky?'

'Well, like . . . it'd be a long time before we could meet again.'

'And that didn't make you think twice?'

'What else can I do? Fishing's my job, isn't it?'

'And you'd sacrifice me just to go and catch a few more fish in a place that's even further away? Is that what you're trying to tell me?'

(The chaperone, who had disappeared off to bed, landed on the table with a crash, sensing sport to be had. *'If you could just hear yourself! You're sounding like a provincial shrew.'*)

'It's my job,' he reiterated as if it was quite obvious. 'There's not a lot of choice in it for me. With this job you just do what's got to be done. That's all there is to it.'

'You could carry on where you are, couldn't you? You're earning quite good money, for the moment.'

'Maybe. But from what I hear it's not going to go on much longer. People prefer battery chicken these days. They don't buy much fish. Even the small trawlers are going through a bad time, and tuna prices are falling. I'm going to have to look for something else.'

'So when is it for this fabulous scheme? I'd quite like to know. Believe it or not, you do count for something in my life.'

'Jesus Christ, do you think it's easy for me? I'm not lucky enough to have a rich family behind me! I've got a son who's an invalid and a wife who's not strong now. I'm not a civil servant, you know. I've got responsibilities, I've got to put them first.'

The angrier he got, the more Breton he sounded. What on earth was she doing with a man whose mind wasn't capable of rising above his pension?

'Listen,' she said. 'It's not always been easy for me either, whatever you think. Would it make you feel better if we dropped it? If we stopped seeing each other altogether?'

'Make me feel better? It would make me feel better in a way.'

Gavin's raw sincerity always took her by surprise.

'Well, so, that makes the situation clear. Obviously I don't mean very much to you, I just make life difficult for you . . .'

Gavin broke in. 'That's not what I said. All I said was it would make me feel better *in a way*. It won't happen all at once, anyway. I don't even know why I told you about it.'

Their bill arrived. Gavin examined it carefully before licking his fingers to count out the notes. As he put his jacket on his expression was grim. George had kept her shawl round her shoulders. You can catch your death of cold in those air-conditioned restaurants.

On their way out they saw a centenarian in his wheelchair, accompanied by his bald wife. George clung instinctively to Gavin's arm, and they made their way back to the motel without exchanging a word. Tomorrow they had to part and already they were feeling orphaned.

'The scheme you know . . . I haven't done anything about it. It's only an idea,' he whispered into George's ear some time later, just before they fell asleep, entwined in each other's arms like a pair of amorous octopuses.

Their alarm call was for five the next morning, not an hour for tender endearments. They didn't even have the same departure times. George was bound for Montreal, stopping off in Boston to see Ellen, who was herself about to go to Jamaica, pelvic floor at the ready. Gavin was leaving for Paris at dawn. He smiled his sad smile as he put on those dreadful sandals with crêpe soles, his patterned cardigan with its front zipper, knitted by Marie-Josée, his seaman's cap. Back in his fisherman's clothes he no longer belonged to George. But did she really want him? During the night her cold sore had blossomed into a veritable bubo, distorting her mouth completely. Feeling so ugly incited her to stop loving Gavin, and she was suddenly impatient to see him go.

He kissed her carefully at the corner of her bottom lip and, for the last time, she clung to the barrel chest which her arms could scarcely surround. Why did she feel like crying every time she parted from this man? He climbed on to the airport bus without looking back. He disapproved of taxis and never let George see him off. Ever since that first parting at Montparnasse, station platforms and departure gates meant 'never more' to him.

George went back to the room to finish her packing, and was just about to go for a last swim when the telephone rang.

'Georch? It's me.'

He hated telephones, and yet he had got through without being able to read a word of the instructions! And he'd had to get hold of cents and quarters, and remember the number of the hotel! George melted.

'Did you ever see a grown man cry in a telephone booth?'

George couldn't speak.

'Well, just look along the wire. And forget everything I said last night. There's another thing I'm going to tell you: it's like a bit of me inside dies every time I leave you. I'm telling you that now, because I wouldn't know how to put it in a letter. Even when I'm hating you I love you. Can you understand that?'

George still couldn't speak for the lump in her throat.

'Georch, are you there? Can you hear me?'

'Yes, it's just that I –'

'Don't worry. It's me that wanted to tell you something for a change. And, do you know, I liked you being angry with me about going to South Africa? Funny but it made me feel as if you were my wife.'

As always, Gavin had such intelligence when he was unhappy. It was when he was relaxed, enjoying himself, making his awful jokes, that George found him stupid. Ah, how sweet love is!

'Right, well, that's it. I've got to be off. No, don't laugh, I know I always say I have to be off but this time it's true. I've got no more change.'

He laughed that laugh she loved. They still had their private passwords, then, their shared allusions and jokes and conspiracies, all those memories of childhood and adolescence too, without which love is only a sexual adventure.

'Write to me.'

They said it at the same time.

8
Vézelay

I was getting ready to marry Gavin. My parents were giving the reception in the drawing room of the Paris apartment, adorned with my father's art collection, not one object of which I recognised. The room looked like an Italian baroque church, stuffed with paintings and gilding and sculptures. Someone was pointing out the most interesting pieces to Gavin, asking if he had any idea how much such and such a vase had cost, telling him it must be twenty thousand dollars at least. 'That rubbish?' Gavin was incredulous. He had no idea what the dollar exchange rate was, but he was outraged, more and more confirmed in his opinion that art was a huge swindle perpetrated by snobs. He was wearing a suit, but he had his seaman's cap on, and I couldn't get through the crowd to tell him to take it off. Behind his back the guests were convulsed with laughter.

I was thinking over and over, 'If we divorce he'll get half of all this 'rubbish' he hates so much. How could I ever have thought this was a good idea?' What's more, he seemed to be smoking a small carved pipe which made him look like an old salt, and it occurred to me that I had never known that he smoked a pipe, he hadn't said anything about it – before.

Then all of a sudden he came over to the far end of the drawing room where I had taken refuge on a low stool, sat down behind me and drew my head on to his chest with such tenderness that I knew: 'That's what it is, now I remember, this is why I'm marrying him.' But it didn't stop me finding the whole business ludicrous. It was a crazy idea to marry at our age, it would have been far better simply to live together.

All sorts of things went on during that party. I met old friends who were astonished at my 'betrayal'. And so on. I could go on telling you for hours . . .

But it would be terribly boring. People's dreams always are. Nothing makes my heart sink more than a friend ringing up in the morning to tell me an extraordinary dream she's had, I'll be amazed . . . 'We were at my place, but I didn't recognise anything . . . Do you know what I mean? I was flying through the air, miles above the town, as if it were the most natural thing in the world. You can't imagine the joy . . .'

But of course we can. Everyone has them, dreams of flying or strange cities, the commonplaces of sleep. And my own dreams are the most commonplace of the lot, so mundane and transparent as to discourage the most obtuse psycho-analyst. I can't think why, beneath my relatively interesting conscious mind, there laps such a pathetic unconscious. But even the most banal dreams can leave a powerful impression, a flavour that lingers for days. Someone comes through time and space to tell you something. Gavin had held me in his arms in that night's dream, and I was sure he had been dream-ing of me at the same moment.

I ached with longing, and wrote him a letter which was much more loving than usual, which I regretted the moment I had posted it. I was aware that it sprang less from wistful-ness for my lover than from wistfulness about the onset of middle age, from a rage to live and rage at the idea of death, from sadness at lost opportunities, a desire to make love, and perhaps because I simply wanted to write the words 'I love you'. I no longer said 'I love you' to Sid.

Yes, I knew what that letter was really saying. I knew too

that Gavin would read every word as gospel. He was too simple to mistrust ladies who wrote stories for a living, or ladies yearning for passionate love and taking refuge in dreams.

During those years, meetings with my cormorant were infrequent and unsatisfactory. I couldn't be at the airport when he flew in from Dakar, because he was always with his crew. He didn't feel able to stay in Paris even for a day or two, because the others left the same day for Lorient and their waiting women. He claimed he couldn't think up a story convincing enough for Marie-Josée, which made me a bit resentful. So all we could manage was lunch together, or occasionally an afternoon. And it wasn't my Gavin I met at these lunches, but Skipper Lozerech, with his seaman's cap and those dreadful knitted cardigans, patterned in front and plain behind (only tourists wear the traditional Breton fishermen's jerseys these days). We were always awkward with each other when our bodies couldn't touch.

I'd tell him about my own travels, though he always irritated me by muddling Napoli and Tripoli or Mount Etna and Mount Fuji. And he would take out his African snaps and proudly show me a photograph of his car, half-hidden by a truck, or the stern of his trawler just showing between cranes at the far end of an inner harbour, or the entrance to a Senegal night club with three blurred silhouettes in front of it ('That's Job, I've told you about him. You don't know the other two.') or the Dakar courthouse, snapped in the rain.

We'd try discussing politics until he'd come out with his standard formulas about all politicians being smooth talkers or a bunch of morons or a right set of bastards, depending on what was in the news at the time.

With nothing but words to sustain us, our intimacy starved, and we found ourselves reduced to social banalities: 'Yvonne's husband's died and she's having trouble with the kids. The second one's been a right bloody fool and got himself put in jug. Our kids are fine, the two oldest at any rate, but they've got so many certificates and diplomas I don't know how to talk to them any more.' This was not the time for me to announce that Loïc, having contemptuously rejected the idea of university, had joined a group of left-wing ecologists who preached not only non-violence but active refusal to do any productive work whatsoever because it polluted the environment and served to enrich our horrible, wasteful consumer society. How could I tell Lozerech our cushy system was to be condemned just as he was beginning to reap its fruits? He went on with the local gossip.

'Old le Floch, you remember him? Father of the le Floch who owns the fishing tackle shop in Concarneau, down by the harbour. Well, he died last month. It comes to us all, *Karedig*.'

'Couldn't you, just for once, not say the obvious?'

'Well, you can't get away from it. Poor old le Floch . . . He didn't suffer, mind. Worse for the ones who are left behind . . . Better off where he is . . .'

He didn't miss a single platitude.

I often wondered why we went on meeting like this; they were such dismal occasions. But Gavin telephoned me every time he was on his way back, and as soon as I knew when he would arrive I dropped everything to be with him. It was as if, through these desolate meetings, we were holding on to a link to some unknown future, for the sake of something secret in the depths of our hearts.

There are certain times in life when you feel that sex is

central. At others it's the intellect, or work, or fame. After
eight or nine years together, Sidney and I had settled into an
affectionate companionship. And, thanks to lack of exercise
or opportunity, my divine madness with Gavin was receding
from my mind. It was my work which took precedence now.
I was enjoying it: I'd accepted a challenging new job, partly
because I was sailing fast towards the Magellan Straits of
my fortieth birthday, and, in my mind, the death-knell of
possibilities was tolling. When you're twenty you want
everything, and you're right to have high hopes. At thirty
you still think you can have everything. At forty it's too late.
It's not that you've aged, it's hope that's aged. Now I knew
I'd never be a doctor, my adolescent dream. Nor, as I'd
thought when I was a child, an Egyptian archaeologist. Nor
a biologist, a great scholar, an anthropologist. Those dreams
had warmed my being and enriched my life, but age gradually makes a desert of them all. Still, I got the chance to touch
on all my favourite subjects when I was offered a job on the
editorial board of a scholarly journal concerned with history
and anthropology.

I was also planning to write a history of women and medicine, which would mean I could fulfil at least some of my
youthful ambitions. The best age, after all, is the one at which
you can see which of your dreams are most important to you
and do something about them. Because working on *Today
and Yesterday*, the journal, meant a lot of travelling, I arranged
a two-year sabbatical from the university.

Things were changing for Gavin too, if not in his personal
life, then in the way he looked at things. The Concarneau
Fisheries Board had finally decided to base some factory ships
in the Seychelles for the tuna fishing, and Gavin had
been given command of one of these floating factories, the

Raguenès. The first six months were very successful, yet, in spite of his reticence, I could tell from Gavin's letters that he was not happy. He felt isolated, at the ends of the earth, because the official language there was English, while Dakar had been an outpost of France, and all his friends there Breton. He made no secret of his longing to come back to France before the Indian Ocean winter, when the seas were lashed by the monsoon.

In France we were having one of those heartbreaking springs when even extinct emotions revive, when you want to be a bird and live in the joy of the moment, however ephemeral. At times like these the lightest breeze can waft you back to being twenty again.

I drove Gavin to Orly airport after one of those lunchtimes which always left me hungry. He was hunched into my little Volkswagen Beetle, taking up all the space with his touching sturdiness, his big knees against the dashboard, his curly head brushing the roof. Those great hands of his, which seemed so huge in the city, aroused more than just memories in me. Our daydreams circulated round the tiny space thickening the air with suppressed desire. I was going to say something but couldn't find the words, when I felt Gavin's hand on my thigh. It was quivering.

'Yes,' I whispered.

And there were so many things in that yes. Yes, I love you but yes, it's too late now, we can't go on playing this game for the rest of our lives, that would become ridiculous, wouldn't it?

He leaned his temple against mine in that sweet familiar gesture, and we drove into the underground car park at the airport without saying a word. Life seemed terribly cruel suddenly, this springtime pointless. While I was parking the car in the third level of that inferno he took my hand brusquely, suddenly overcome by the feeling that he couldn't leave me the way he'd done those other times.

'I'm sorry, I shouldn't be saying this, but sometimes I can't stand never seeing you. I mean . . . I do see you but . . . Oh, you know what I mean. Look, I've got an idea. I'm not sure when we're going back to Mahé, not the exact date anyway, but I think I can manage five days or so just before. The ship will be in for a refit, and they're sure to run late. We could be together then if you like . . . if you can get away. If you want to of course.'

If I wanted to. I ran my eyes over him to remind myself of everything I loved: his buccaneer's face, youthful again with revived hope, those curling eyelashes with the sun-bleached tips, that mouth on which, so often, I had known the taste of eternity. I was overcome with a kind of weariness at the thought of embarking on yet another of those bouts of fever which, like all the others, would have to be stifled, chilled before I would be able to return to normal life. Weren't we too old for these games?

'Don't say anything yet,' said Gavin, guessing what was going through my mind. 'I know already what you're about to say. I'd agree hundred per cent with anyone who told me it'd be best to put an end to all this. But,' he said simply, 'it's too strong for me.' And he stroked my face with his rough gentle hand while his beautiful husky-dog eyes darkened with tenderness. 'Times when I see you, I can't accept I've lost you. It's wrong, I know, but I think of you as my real wife, the one I wanted from the start.'

With the speed of light, the speed of memory, emotion flooded my body which, until then, had been curbed. Spring suddenly came all the way down into the third level of that underground car park. And I can never resist spring.

'So we're going to start all over again with this? We're going to risk being unhappy again?'

'Sod that, I don't care about being unhappy. It's the thought of never being *happy* that . . .'

'Lozerech mine, we don't have time to go on about love. Have you seen the time? Just let me look at my diary.'

As it happened, I was due to do an article about an old settlement of Gauls which was being reconstructed in Burgundy. Why not risk a cultural holiday with Gavin, take him there, to Vézelay, for instance. All at once, I was thrilled by the thought of love.

'Suppose for the first time I asked you to be my guest, in France? I'll be on expenses myself, so a double room makes no difference. We could enjoy good food, some history and everything . . .'

'I'm all in favour of the everything bit. But I'll do the history too if I must. You'll be sorry.'

He hugged me with all the force he could manage in that tiny space, grabbed his bag and went off with that rolling gait of his which had made me weak at the knees so many years before. As I drove back up to the daylight, I even breathed the air of the hangars and motorways with joy, wondering how I had survived without this intense feeling of life.

So, a few weeks later, it was in the heart of France, for once, I met my cormorant again. A strangely dejected cormorant, trailing his wings, as if mutilated by an oil slick. Even the pleasure of having me to himself wasn't enough to hide his uneasiness and apprehension at the thought of his imminent departure for the Seychelles.

'Four days, it's too short. It's worse than nothing,' he said to excuse his nerviness when he climbed into the car. 'I'm not used to living so fast like that.'

For the first time since I had seen him standing bare-chested on the farm cart, surrounded by ripe sheaves, and had been devastated (a love which lasts for twenty years is a sort of devastation), he was no longer the victorious centaur, impervious to sorrow and the marks of time. His eyes seemed smaller, less vividly blue, and there was grey in the astrakhan curls at his temples. The skin of his face seemed distended and worn, and the bumps and hollows around his eyes were deep as the parallel lines on his forehead. For the first time, beneath those handsome features, you could guess at the old man he would become.

We drove out of Paris in my faithful Beetle on one of the delusive late summer days when everything hints at treachery though you can't see any proof. Autumn lurked behind a profusion of asters, dahlias, chrysanthemums, and a mock spring of roses and wisteria, and bided its time. But the earth lay scored by the plough, exposed, its crops razed, its mop of weeds shaved. Only the vineyards of Burgundy were preparing to live their hour of glory.

Was it this presentiment of winter which always subtly poisoned late summer for me? Or was it the endless distance between Gavin's life and mine, now that he even breathed the air of another hemisphere, four degrees below the Equator? The safety ropes we threw to each other now fell into the void, and something harder than absence lodged between us.

We drove two hundred miles without being able to reach each other. I couldn't find my place in his life. Did I have one, anyway, outside of illusion? He too seemed ill at ease, but I knew he hated being cooped up in a car. He was as restless as a caged bear, stretching and twisting his neck from side to side, as if to unscrew his head from his shoulders, crossing and uncrossing his legs not knowing where to put them, shifting his bottom on the seat, probably because his trousers were constricting his private parts. He was so like a tiresome child I almost expected to hear wails of 'Mummee, how much longer? Mummee, are we nearly there?' But his broad hand rested on my thigh like a vow. And Gavin was always true to his vows. We found ourselves unable, though, to establish that total truce of our other trips which had made us forget our ordinary lives the moment we saw each other. So low was he that he almost confessed to needing love, and the smallest gesture of tenderness brought tears to his eyes. He no longer made love as if devouring a feast or champing at the bit or, simply, drawing breath. Now he flung himself on it, as if plunging into water or trying to get drunk or taking revenge. With a kind of rage he chose me to witness what was tormenting him, as he tried to free himself of something stifling. The word 'depression' had never figured in his vocabulary, nor, therefore, in his life. 'Feeling down' was laughably inadequate. He wasn't able to speak of existential anguish so all he did was repeat, 'I'm not feeling myself.'

His work was a lot harder now than it had been in Senegal or the Ivory Coast, and the brief landfalls much less fun than in Dakar where he had so many friends from Brittany and the Vendée and the Basque country. And the Seychelles, such lotus-eating lands for everyone else, made him worry about the decision he had come to. What's more, he was at sea for a month at a time, 'a whole hellish month', with a crew of thirty Frenchmen and three blacks who, said Gavin, did less between them than one cabin boy from Brittany.

For the first time in his life he found his certainties eroded. That's what exhausted him. He was a man who couldn't exist without his certainties, nor was he capable of modifying them. Every day he went over his problems obsessively, even as we savoured our Escargots de Bourgogne or our Fricassée of Wild Mushrooms in the great gastronomic restaurants of the region, and at night, after we had made love, when he couldn't get to sleep.

I was learning something about his sense of pride. He couldn't bear not being respected for his work any more. You could ask him to die rescuing a ship in distress, but not to question what, for him, made his life's work different from any other.

'Them Seychellese, they just laugh at us slaving away. They think it's bloody stupid to come all that way, in boats that cost millions, working our guts out to send tins of tuna to the French who've got more than enough to eat anyway. And do you have any idea what these boats cost?'

No, I did not. What's more, I did not necessarily want to know, not at two a.m. on our first night together. What I wanted was to sleep – or to make love again, or to talk sweet, silly pillow-talk, but not to learn the price of a factory boat, delivery to Mahé included. Especially as I was expected to exclaim 'How much! You must be joking!' when, with a touch of pride, he named a sum so huge that, even wide awake, I shouldn't have been able to grasp it.

'So you see. It's endless worry for the Fisheries Board. And for us. It's not the work that kills you, it's the worry. There you are, in charge of a whole load of electronic equipment which costs god knows what. And it's a disaster when anything breaks down. It costs the Board a fortune every day we can't work. Us too. We don't get paid if there's no fish. And just try getting anything repaired out there. They've no idea of work, lazy buggers. Not one of them. And in the end, it's us who look like idiots.'

'Well, in a way, maybe that's what you are.'

'Could be. But it's the only way I know, and that's the bloody problem. I couldn't change even if I wanted to. I don't know how to do anything else.'

I said it wasn't so and I told him that I loved what he did and that I loved even more the way that he did it. I slipped into the role of sweet young story-book Bécassine, incapable of understanding the tough life of men and wanting only one thing – to be petted. That kind of attitude usually comforted him. Maybe that kind of woman too? He needed silliness. So, finally, the Little Woman and the Big Man made love.

When I was young, with a certain sense of humiliation, I'd identified less with little Bécassine than with Montherlant's Andrée Hacquebaut, abandoned on the doormat in front of the beloved Master's house. It was the time when Montherlant imperiously classified young girls into two categories – the ravishing ones to whom he refused any claim to intelligence, and the intelligent ones, who could never, in his view, be beautiful. In this way he relegated them to the outer darkness, far from his divine phallus. I was quite accustomed to playing both the intellectual harpy and the submissive princess for Gavin. And for the moment, the princess was in the ascendant, cherishing him and prattling away to make him forget about the sea. But the sea would always come crashing back and we found ourselves scudding off on the Indian Ocean again, as it lapped against the very foundations of the Hôtel de la Poste at Vézelay.

'What's so hard', resumed Gavin, as if our love-making had been nothing but a brief intermission, 'is that what we're at doesn't have anything to do with real fishing. It's that different. You hardly ever get to see the fish. The minute they're caught, they're gutted and chucked straight into the freezers. And there you are, slaving away, just like in a factory. They'll be catching tuna ready-tinned before long.'

The princess had had it up to here with tuna. The bloody things had joined them in the car, had been at their every meal and excursion, had even climbed into bed with them. All I could do was curl up in Lozerech's arms and put in a word now and then, given that there wasn't a hope of sleep. But what words could be adequate? It was so difficult not to view his life with my landlubber's assumptions, not to apply my own standards of comfort and health and well-being, which don't apply at all. Even the most ordinary objects – a bed, a bookcase – have different meanings at sea, where everything is distorted by the ocean's monstrous parameters.

'And yet, when you were just starting out, in the Irish Sea, I remember you telling me it was as bad as convict labour. It must be better in the Tropics, isn't it? You don't have to sleep in those coffin-bunks, do you? And you've got showers and all that sort of thing?'

'It's worse than being a convict somehow.'

Defeated by the difficulty of explaining, he gave up. All he could say was 'I don't know how to describe it. No one could,' before lapsing into silence, haunted by images untranslatable into words. Sneakily, I started drifting off. But Gavin hadn't finished his monologue yet. Hands behind his head, he kept one of his legs over mine to assure me that his body was with me, even if his thoughts weren't.

'Can't complain about the weather, that's for sure. But it's not the weather that's the trouble. At least I was a real trawlerman then. Now it isn't like you're catching fish, it's like fishing for banknotes. The machinery's the skipper now. And, like I say, I'm just a factory hand.'

'A factory hand who works in the middle of the ocean, with the wind and the waves.'

'What waves? You can't even hear them!' He laughed bitterly. 'I'd like to see you putting up with it, even for a week. There are engines going twenty-four hours a day. Engines for the freezer-rooms where we put the fish. Engines making ice for the vats of brine. Just imagine what that's like when it's a hundred and twenty degrees outside. On top of that, there's the ship's engines, two thousand horsepower. Oh, and the helicopter spotting the shoals. That's a racket if you like. In the end you don't know where you are, and you don't know what's worse: the engine room where it's a hundred and thirty degrees or the freezer-rooms where there's ice on the walls. And even when you're back in port, there's still the noise of the air-conditioning, and the noise of the crane that lifts the containers out of the hold. They weigh a couple of tons apiece. What I'm used to is carrying the fish crates myself, catching tuna with my own lines. I don't like being at the beck and call of a machine. No, you have to be mad, to work in conditions like that. In any case, I'm getting too old. And soon there'll be no tuna left . . . Oh, sod it. I'll be retired by then.'

I wasn't going to get any sleep. Resigned, I put the light on. It was a wonderfully soft night, and we went to lean from the window of our little room under the eaves, looking out on to the jumbled roofs of Vézelay and the quiet hills beyond. Before Gavin lay a silent countryside, the rural peace he must sometimes have dreamed of on stormy nights. For the first time since I had known him, he took a cigarette from his jacket pocket and turned to me.

'Do you mind? It calms my nerves.'

'You're really wretched out there, aren't you?'

'I wouldn't say that.'

It was always the same. He hated making too much of his suffering. That night, not even making love could help him. What he needed was sympathy, a good listener.

Next day some of his cares seemed to have lifted. We had a picnic lunch of bread and sausage, cheese, and fruit, and I dragged him off to various old piles of stone, as he called them. This was the first time we had seen France together, and normally he would have enjoyed it. I used every history teacher's trick on him, told him about men with whom he could identify like Vauban, his Vauban, who was buried here, in a little chapel which he'd had built, far from his and Gavin's sea, in the foundations of the Château of Bazoches which, like almost every other building in these parts, dated from the twelfth century.

We took long walks in the deeply rural landscape with its constant, consoling reminders of the past, which gradually calmed my sea bird. But, although his face regained some of its childhood quality, his eyes weren't as vividly blue as I had known them. Some sea eyes go pale inland. It's when they reflect the blue of the ocean that they have their full force.

The third evening – and already our penultimate one – Gavin sensed my sadness at the thought of the long months of separation ahead, and at the fate of a love which neither wanted to fully live nor to die completely, so he came up with a sudden inspiration.

'There's something I want to ask you.' We were finishing

one of those meals so exquisite that eating them makes you feel superior. 'Would you think of joining me in Mahé again? We'll be through just before the monsoon, and I could probably manage a short time then. It's a long way for sure . . .' He sighed. 'I never stop thinking about you there, about the way you were, the way *we* were, together. It's not the same place without you. It's just . . . If I knew you were coming, it wouldn't be so bad leaving next week.'

'It's the most beautiful memory of my life, that time in the Seychelles with you. But . . .'

Gavin interrupted to stop me from raising objections. 'I don't like to ask. The trip's really pricey, I know. But they opened an international airport last July, so it's a lot easier. And Conan would lend us his house. You remember him? He's been a project worker there since independence. It wouldn't cost you a penny once you're there. It'll all be on me, for as long as you want to stay. There's the flight of course, I couldn't manage that. But think about it. If you did come, it would be our twentieth anniversary, remember? We could celebrate it on the *Raguenès*, so we'd feel at home, at least.'

'*Twenty years and you'd still go eight thousand miles for Monsieur Lozerech's sex organ. That works out pretty expensive per ounce,*' said the chaperone.

Yes, so expensive that it didn't make sense. I sat there, not knowing what to think, but then Gavin covered my hand with one of his, that great unwieldy paw which never knew where to put itself. His hands always looked orphaned unless working on a boat or on me.

'The flight's not cheap and it's long. Over twenty-four hours, isn't it? But I might manage it if my book goes well. I could try to get an advance from the publisher. Loïc spends the summer holidays with his father, so there's no problem there. Look, I'll find out about flights, there may be some bargains. I'll let you know . . .'

Gavin could see I was still hesitating.

'Try to come. Please.' Those simple words finished me. He had given me everything yet asked nothing of me. And he had so needed me to say yes. Right there and then. The unhappiness he so rarely allowed himself to show moved me deeply. I felt that by continuing to love Gavin I was obeying a very pure emotion, for only a love so true could explain why we were never discouraged by all the obstacles in our path. Think how much easier it would have been to love a man who was learned, elegant, rich, free, intelligent and living in Paris.

As soon as Gavin was sure of me, my promise tucked warm and safe within him, we became lighthearted again. On the drive back to Paris we were like an old couple who, though they know that life will soon part them for a while, are sure of their future together.

'We'll have a great party for our anniversary,' he promised. 'That's one thing they do know how to do out there. We'll ask Youn if you like, my second-in-command. He knows all the best places in the islands. He's got a girl too, in Lorient. They've been in love for ages. But his wife's in the asylum, so he can't get a divorce.'

I had a discomfiting thought. What on earth would I do if Gavin's wife were to die? Neglected wives can't have the least idea how much their existence is the very condition which favours illicit love. Wronged wives are buttresses against reality for husbands who would be desperate if they had to face the truth. It was thanks to Marie-Josée, both what she was and what she failed to be, that I could love Gavin without having to reject him a second time.

Being in a car, especially a tiny one like mine, is like returning to the security of the womb. There we were, Gavin and I, curled up in our little cell, safe from the world. As always when about to part, we found ourselves needing reassurance about this love which, even at the most perfect and intense moments, never let us forget its contradictory side.

'Did you see that our little cottage on the island at Raguenès has collapsed? We wouldn't be able to shelter there now. Just think. We probably wouldn't be here together if it had collapsed twenty years earlier.'

'It was fate. I know it. You won't ever make me think otherwise,' Gavin declared. It was probably because his life at sea was so chancy that he hated to admit chance into the rest of his life.

Like children, lovers need to go over the same old stories time after time. Tell me the one about the boy and girl who sheltered on the island . . . Once again we went over every detail of that improbable night in 1950, which even now hadn't yielded up every last secret. Once again I begged him to tell me about his love–hate for the little daughter of the summer visitors next door. Once again he wanted to know what I saw in the yokel who'd been so sure that I waltzed in Paris every night, under sparkling chandeliers with juvenile leading men in white tie and tails. Little did he know that my suitor was a maths student with spots and spectacles, whose Moroccan rug just didn't compare to the mud floor of our cottage and the smell of our beach at low tide.

The car radio was playing old songs, and Gavin sang along with every one of them. The radio means so much to sailors – one more thing that Gavin missed in the Seychelles – and he'd listened so often that he knew all the lyrics, which were glorified by that voice which hadn't changed since the day it had inoculated me with a love philtre at Yvonne's wedding.

See you in eight months in Victoria, *Karedig*?

9
Arise, Free Men!

Sidney and I had had a difficult winter. His novel had been as total a failure as he could have hoped. But it's one thing to be an admirer of doomed authors and to respect only those who don't seek success, quite another to endure public indifference, and not a single review. You need the sort of strength, and scorn for ordinary mortals, which Sidney lacked. Not to mention financial security, which he had forfeited by leaving the States.

My two books, on the other hand, were unexpectedly successful considering they were historical studies published by an academic press, and this made for a subtle shift in our relationship. I was more interesting to him now that he was less interesting to other people, though he persisted in regarding my books as good only for earning an honest crust. All the same we were getting to an age (Sidney had just turned fifty) when an honest crust has its charms.

I found myself thinking about Gavin a lot of the time then. A dark blue seaman's cap on a sailor's head in a harbour, the sound of a Breton voice on a Concarneau street, my visits to Madame Lozerech – who was dwindling quietly every year on her abandoned farm, all her children away, teaching or at sea – and I would feel a sudden wave of tenderness for the little boy who had punctured my bicycle tyres and shouted rude rhymes. I was like the wife of a prisoner, my life suspended while I waited for him. Sleeping beside Sidney, I dreamed of someone else. A sex which is bored amuses itself by dreaming up nameless transports. Shameless how it's dreams can come true as well!

I set about organising my trip. Was it age that made me go to the Seychelles, not just to see Gavin, but to bask in a lover's gaze? Unnourished by the love in his eyes, my skin was parched and withering. And then, I could see how my mother, in spite of all her efforts, was gradually giving in to age, surrendering the things and territories she loved, pretending to lose interest so as not to admit defeat. There comes a time when you cannot recapture the territory you have lost. But she still had enough of that appetite for life which I admired so much to offer me a piece of advice:

'Think very carefully about what you'd lose if you gave up your Breton friend. [That was her tactful name for him.] Nothing can take the place of passion. Intellect is all very well, but it doesn't do anything for your body. The trouble is that women like us need them both,' she said with an air of false regret. She had never cared for Sidney.

I had persuaded François and Luce to join me for my third week in the Seychelles, if Luce's health permitted, so that we could fly back together. I had told them so much about the islands that they were bent on seeing them. Luce had recently undergone surgery and was going through a course of chemotherapy, but so gallant and optimistic was she that we allowed ourselves to hope that this remission might be a genuine cure.

When I arrived at last in Mahé, the Seychelles were celebrating the first anniversary of their independence, and we made the most of their festivities that mirrored our own. We behaved like an old married couple returning to a place full of happy memories. 'Do you remember the centipede sting? And that dreadful family on Praslin with their *coco-fesse*?' The questions lovers ask to reassure themselves.

We spent the first evening dancing under the palm trees and in every nightclub and restaurant in the place. The British presence, officially departed, could be felt everywhere. At midnight a band, as stiff and starched as when they had played 'God Save the Queen', struck up the new national anthem of the Seychelles:

> Aris', free men! Proud Seschelese!
> Equality fo' yoh an' me
> An libahty fo' all our lan's.

Evidently they had not forgotten the French influence, with its lofty revolutionary principles.

I embellished the anthem for our own purposes, and sang to Gavin:

> 'Aris', free spar, proud Concarnois!'

adding our own bawdy note to the patriotic strains.

Our anniversary ended at dawn, in the warm ocean. But we were not as diffident on that shore as we had been twenty years ago. Only the very young can afford the luxury of self-denial.

Should I describe those days – days which we treated as nights every time it rained? (The chaperone: *'Spare us. We've already been subjected to your interminable Seychelles routine. Sex, when it's not so exciting any more, gets to be disgusting. There's no middle ground.'*)

By the third day Gavin had burst a blood vessel in his left eye. It didn't hurt, but every time I looked at it I felt like a ghoul who had given her male lover an ocular thrombosis with her insatiable demands. Even so, there was no holding me; it was as if I were incapable of switching off. The engine might flood sometimes, but it never stalled. Like a gardener's green fingers, Gavin's 'blue' fingers – the blue of jokes and movies – made my body blossom, discovering places of desire I'd never known before. Some of these were fleeting and felt only once, others had the effect of total eclipses. Then there were the trustworthy places which, like a stave of music, produced the same melody every time. Gavin questioned me about them but I could never be sure of locating those shifting frontiers for him, so knocked out was I with sensations, not all of which might have counted as true orgasms in Ellen's strict taxonomy.

'I wish you'd tell me what you really like,' Gavin pleaded. 'There must be something you don't like to ask for.'

'I can't think of anything much, I promise. Anyway, if you knew absolutely everything about the way I responded you wouldn't be you any more, you'd be me. That would be awful.'

'But I don't even know exactly when you come, usually. That bothers me. I wonder then if I've . . .'

'Don't wonder at all. Ask me. If you think about it, sex isn't as purely sexual as it's cracked up to be. No one has ever given me what you give me, not just pleasure, but a sense of the sacred in pleasure.'

I had hardly dared say that. But it was dark, and Gavin didn't object. He wasn't scared of big questions. And, with him, I wasn't scared of anything. With Gavin I could give free rein to my wildest fantasies, could sing and dance when he was around as freely as I could alone. I flaunted clothes which I would have to hide carefully when I got back to ordinary life. There was a satin blouse, for instance, which cried out to be torn off me, and which I should never have dreamed of buying at home. Oh, those female tricks which I despise and condemn but which reaped me such a rich reward with him!

I even went on board Gavin's boat as a wife might have done, to be shown his cabin, and the bunk where he slept, and the place where he hid my letters and photographs. And, when the *Raguenès* sailed, I was on the quay waving and running down to the end to watch that dear form grow fainter among the others on deck, like all the women in every seaport the world over. And, like all the women seeing their sailor off the world over, my eyes misted over.

It was lucky that François and Luce had arrived the day before and that we'd all spent the evening together, down by the port. Gavin was comfortable with them, and I was happy too, knowing that they didn't see him as some 'noble savage' from the provinces but simply as someone who led a different kind of life. Some of my friends who would accord respect and interest to an Eskimo or a Turk had scarcely dissembled their condescending boredom when Lozerech talked about the sea. Not only was his accent a joke but Brittany was too close to home to count as exotic enough for them.

François wasn't like that at all. He cut through superficial differences of class and education to get to the man's real qualities. There we sat, all four of us round a restaurant table, and for once, with my friends, Gavin wasn't made to feel like 'that yokel George had picked up'.

Gavin and I promised to write to each other, using Conan's address, although we knew that weeks might pass between his getting a letter from me, or sending one. The sea deprived him of another comfort too, one which even prisoners are permitted, which was hearing a loved one's voice.

In his first letter he confessed to something he'd not told me in Mahé: he was giving up the Seychelles tuna fishing and was going to do his famous South African project he'd been so mysterious about. It was only for three or four years, till he retired. It wasn't the end of the world!

Oh no? Four years was an eternity to me; trawlermen have a totally different concept of time, of course, since there are no forty-hour weeks or even weekends or bank holidays in their lives. Once more I felt discouraged by our refugee love, always second to his wife and family, and no sooner revived than it had to be smothered again. What's more, my own grand project occupied my thoughts. François, who was a gynaecologist and obstetrician, could now collaborate on my historical study of women and medicine, and his specialised knowledge would be immensely helpful. Besides, I was beginning to realise how perfectly my life suited me. I could spend my own money, see friends, travel whenever I chose, live in a flat I liked. Gavin would be an old man before he reaped any rewards from his years of thankless toil and went to live in that 'nice' house for good – by which time he would have lost any idea of how to live on terra firma. What a gulf there truly was between my existence and that of a Lozerech!

So it was that, as the months went by, Gavin became a silhouette on the horizon in spite of our regular letters. I sincerely tried to free myself of him. The heart, however, has its own secret agenda, and soon it wasn't Gavin but Sidney I felt freed of. The intellectual kit that came with him hardly concerned me any more. I'd thrown it off, away. When I acquired the nasty habit of comparing my two men, I realised that Sidney had never thought of my body as unique or of me as irreplaceable. With good reason, actually. But I had known what it was to have somebody feel wild about me, and good reasoning didn't seem so appealing now.

Those first years in the States I had felt flattered by being included in the avant-garde, with their erotic ways. I had actually believed in an avant-garde for love! With Al and Ellen Price and our other friends – psychotherapists, sex-therapists, sexologists, all of them – we had brilliant discussions about love and sex. Not that it helped us much in practice. After the publication of Ellen's book Al became impotent except with prostitutes. And Sidney threw himself passionately into the experiment of sex with a multiplicity of partners. His relaxed dilettantism, which I had once thought so enviable, now seemed more pathological than enlightened.

I was recognising that, as a relationship progresses, every-thing depends on the way you look at things. A lover's behaviour can move you or madden you depending on whether you're looking for reasons to stay or reasons to leave. Those days everything about Sidney maddened me. That was when he decided he wanted to marry me, whereas I had lost any desire to be his wife. Why change my name to an American one at my age anyway! I jibbed at the thought of growing old and therefore devoted, devotion being man-datory in the marriage contract. Sidney, at this time, was at his sweetest and most considerate. Strange how when one partner is down the other is so often up.

It sometimes takes just one cruel insight to know that it's all over. For me it was the night that Sidney gazed at me after making love, full of gratitude, and said, 'There's so much tenderness in your eyes!' In fact, I had spent the entire time thinking about a pair of shoes I'd seen in a shop window, and cursing myself for not having bought them. I had just the moment he spoke decided to go and get them as soon as I could decently climb out of bed.

And that is how, in one year, I detached myself from both the men in my life – completely from Sidney since he had to return to the States, less completely from Gavin, for

10
The Roaring Fifties

plateau, which, though rising only three hundred feet above the sea, plunged over fifteen thousand below, to a seabed teeming with crayfish. Before he left, Gavin gave me a chart of the area on which he had sketched his old ninety-foot tuna boat *Empire of the Seas*, so I could locate this pathetic scrap of life lost in the infinite blue wastes. His cousin Youn, from one of those Douarnenez families which had specialised in crayfish through the generations, had been the first to discover this rich trove, and decided to exploit it, which meant of course virtually living there. But he had cracked one of his cervical vertebrae in a fishing accident and never fully recovered. So he had to offer this gold mine to a buccaneer like himself. Not many men would have taken it on, but Lozerech had always been drawn to the impossible. He saw in it a chance to relive the intensity of his youth and to end his career in a blaze of glory. Also, possibly, a chance to put yet another obstacle in the way of our love. Since he couldn't diminish his feelings, he chose to increase the distance between. And he had found yet another reason for punishing himself: Marie-Josée, like Luce, had had an operation for cancer. 'They took everything out,' she would announce, her bitter tone betraying an awareness that she'd been a womb and nothing else. Even so, what remained of her was still the wife of Lozerech, and his guilt was even worse.

The book on women and medicine had been published at last. François and I had spent three years on it alongside our other activities, three years of work so all-consuming that its end left us both feeling strangely empty. At first we put this down to our now having so much unaccustomed free time we didn't know what to do with but, as the weeks passed, we both came to realise that what we were missing was that daily companionship which we had enjoyed for so long. The solution was simple: we must live together. Luce had died, and François was alone with his fifteen-year-old daughter. I saw him distraught with all his teaching, and the babies to be delivered, and an adolescent daughter and, above all, his grief for the exceptional woman he had loved so deeply.

It can be a delightful adventure choosing to live with someone simply out of tenderness after having tried a marriage for better or for worse and having lived a so-called carnal passion. François and I had reached an age when love is everything, of course, but, at the same time, it's not everything, a paradox which helps explain the combination of frivolity and seriousness with which we decided to get married. In taking what was really quite a grave risk I didn't feel I was embarking on anything new. François had always been part of the family, and this was simply making it official. There had been various points in our lives when we had just missed falling in love with each other. I might well have married him in 1950 if he hadn't, right in the middle of his studies, been whisked into a TB sanatorium for two years. By the time he returned I was married to Jean-Christophe. As our divorce came through, François and Luce got married. Five years later, when Luce was on the point of leaving him, I was living with Sidney in the States. But here we were, free and healthy at the same time, and we made the most of it. Lozerech would never have been part of my life, let alone my memories, if I had married François when I was twenty, but Jean-Christophe had never satisfied my capacity for love. He had left a space for my longings and my adolescent memories. That's how some men make the bed in which their rivals will sleep.

François was a rare being: one of those great men who don't quite make it. With his gifts he could have been a famous academic, a poet, a painter, a pianist, a Casanova. He almost became all these, but tiny weaknesses of character or a series of chances perhaps, kept him just on the wrong side of success, a state of affairs with which he seemed perfectly content. Although not conventionally handsome, he had a delightful physical presence and an innate style. He had just enough diffidence and casualness to earn people's forgiveness for those gifts which had got him nicknamed Boy Wonder when he was young. He was still young in fact, though over fifty, because he was fascinated by everything. He brought each baby into the world as if it were all the world to him; he was passionate about his friends, music, travel, his daughter Marie and now our marriage, which seemed to be part of the natural order of things to him. In spite of all the sickness and death he had witnessed, he regarded the universe as fundamentally good. He loved life and, more unusually, the living. He even loved my affair with Lozerech, whom he nicknamed 'Captain Cormorant', after one of the heroes of the books we had shared in childhood.

I pinned Gavin's map on my study wall, and never looked at it without that tiny boat tugging at my heart-strings. He had drawn it with the care and precision he brought to everything, so that it had its derrick, its mizzen mast, its small brown stay-sail. My cormorant was lost out there with his crew of eight and seven hundred lobster pots to be drawn up, re-baited and lowered back into the sea on lines up to three hundred feet long. He was in that boat on an ocean swarming with octopus and monstrous moray eels, and churned by terrible storms uninterrupted by any land mass. At least that is how I imagined it from reading books by men who had navigated those hostile waters, and from the log which Gavin regularly sent me.

Several times, during those long absences of his, I visited Marie-Josée, vaguely looking to breathe in something of him. But seeing his wife and house made me even more aware of the distance which separated us, on land as well as by sea. I couldn't believe I was the Other Woman of a man who planned to end his days in this soulless setting, who would eat his meals in a kitchen fitted out in so-called country style – as Marie-Josée proudly pointed out. She didn't remark that she had rejected some real country furniture at their parents' homes because she considered it old tat, not for well-off people. My Gavin would sleep beside this woman, with her greying hair and sweaty smell, under this pink satin counterpane, his wedding pictures and the portraits of both sets of parents in oval carved frames on the wall above his head. From that bed he would be faced by this overglossed reproduction chest of drawers, chosen from a catalogue, on which stood a cheap crystal vase holding five silver plastic ferns and three purple plastic tulips.

But what had my Gavin in common with Lozerech? No more than I had in common with the woman who had journeyed right to the end of the world (chaperone hard on her heels) to find that mysterious thrill that is based on nothing that human language can convey. All of us have our facets like that cut-glass vase of Marie-Josée's.

During the first two years of the four he planned to spend on the fishing bank Lozerech earned more money than he had during the whole of his career hitherto. Once his huge salt-water tanks were full, he made for the Cape to unload his tons of crayfish which were then airlifted, live, to a Lorient wholesaler. He didn't have a life at all in any real meaning of the word. All he did was take soundings, watch the lines, try not to go mad in that heaving emptiness, and look forward to retirement.

The crayfish had transformed the family fortunes. The crayfish had built an extension to the house, sent the eldest son to the States to get his master's degree in chemistry, paid for a specially adapted car for the disabled Joël. One of Gavin's daughters was a teacher in Rennes, the other was an air hostess. Marie-Josée sported three gold teeth. They had reason to be grateful to the crayfish.

I hesitated about telling Gavin that I had married François. I took the plunge in the end, in case he heard it first from Marie-Josée. He would, I knew, see it as a kind of betrayal, even though it was he who had chosen to put such a distance between us. It was a long time before he wrote again, either because of jealousy or out of a sense of decency towards François, whom he liked a lot. And perhaps it was out of my own sense of decency towards François, not that he ever asked it of me, that I started thinking of Gavin in the past tense.

Then something happened to change all this. My mother died. She was knocked over by a van on the corner of a Paris boulevard. Mama had always crossed the road as if she were still in the horse-drawn era, never bothering with crossings or traffic lights, but simply raising her hand confidently to stop the oncoming carriages. But the horsepower of the van was unable to stop in time. She died of multiple injuries a few days later, still fulminating against the way people drove these days. At sixty-eight, in brilliant health, she had firmly intended to live on a good few years yet, so I had always put off the knowledge that some day I should have to live my life without her. Now, sitting by her bed, watching over her final coma, I realised with horror that never again, for the rest of my life, would I be able to say 'Hello, Mama.' By disappearing she took from me the first word I had learned, a word which had been the rock on which my life was built. Leaving without warning is a mother's first, sometimes her only, betrayal. Tears sprang to my eyes every time François said 'your mama'. From this time forward it was a word I tried to avoid.

I wrote to tell Gavin. I knew I could talk to him about my mother. She had boxed his ears and called him a 'little ruffian' so often that he retained a soft spot for her all his life.

Her death made me take a hard look at my life. I realised that there was one person left in the world who loved me unconditionally and that I risked losing him as well if I continued to do nothing. The day he retired our love would have to be buried. I could not bear to think of him as just one of my collection of memories. My marriage to François was sweet harmony, but still, deep within, was the girl who had run to the island at Raguenès, who had run to the ends of the world to find that 'flame' which makes love the opposing pole to death . . . I knew my mother would have approved. Avid for everything life could offer, never resigned to losing any of it, she would have reminded me that to be faithful to oneself one, sometimes, has to be unfaithful to others. That was one of her principles.

I had the perfect opportunity. Every autumn I lectured for a month at the University of Montreal, where I had the loan of a small apartment with plenty of room for a guest. The year before Loïc, who had some programmes to do for Canadian television, had stayed with me. But the hardest thing would be to inspire Gavin with enough courage to lie to his wife. She was – with good reason – querulous and suspicious. It is hard for a fisherman to think of spending his rare leaves anywhere but with his family.

In my letter, I told him how my mother's death had changed the way I looked at things. Explaining that made me realise how very much I needed to see him. I did all I could to reopen his wounds, twisting the knife until his one desire would be to hold me in his arms, to submit once again to the fever which made him lose all sense of right and wrong.

He was deeply moved that my bereavement should make me need him. Our letters, which had begun in a mood of nostalgia, grew increasingly tender and became, finally, so passionate that we couldn't accept the idea of a future without those moments outside time which had given our lives a dimension neither of us could define, but which we both knew was vital to us.

Love letters are a refined form of love-making. Each note, each of his rare telephone calls, each word of love, seemed a victory over age and death. I thoroughly enjoyed bringing Gavin to the state of arousal, physical and emotional, which would make him think that it was he who had taken the initiative to meet again. And, in his letters, the depth of his feelings more than made up for his awkwardness of expression. This man who tried to live only by the precepts of duty and the dignity of labour became a poet when he wrote to me. He called me his life, his truth, his very breath.

Six months after my mother's death we decided to meet in Montreal the following autumn, just before his winter season. He couldn't pretend that it was too expensive now: he was earning enough money not to feel guilty about keeping back the price of a plane ticket to Canada. Although he didn't admit it, he was already anxious about returning to the world of land-dwellers. He knew that an old salt has no idea of what to do in the real world, and soon ages. That fear inspired him to invent an excuse so unexpectedly bold that Marie-Josée was silenced. He told her he was going to look at the great Canadian north with a mate from Quebec he'd met at the Cape who'd asked him to stay. A flagrant lie often works much better than the most elaborately realistic alibi.

Happy though I was with François, the plan once made, I became childishly elated. My life was coloured with romance again, and I felt twenty years younger.

Paradoxically, I shared more of Gavin's life than ever during those years, because he had got into the habit of writing me a few lines almost every evening, once anchored off some corner of the reef where the sea broke a little less savagely. He would write of each day's happenings whenever the weather, habitually foul, became what he called manageable – it was never, ever good. Every time they put in at the Cape he would send a little parcel of those scraps of ruled paper of his. As the weeks went by, these despatches from South Africa accumulated into an astonishing account, artless, free of pretensions, telling of hell on that coral reef which he saw simply as his place of work, his open-cast mine. His straightforwardness and modest reticence so contrasted with the violence of the elements he described. There was the loneliness (which I guessed weighed heavily on him), the perpetual exhaustion, the storms making chronically bad weather even worse, the accidents. Horror scenes too, like when one of the men, in a diving-suit, had to plunge right to the bottom of the salt-water tanks, through the swarming crayfish, to collect the dead ones which might contaminate the whole precious cargo. His little pages added up to a moving account, which would have graced my own journal or the anthropological magazine *Terre des Hommes*. François, to whom I read some of the best bits, suggested it to Gavin one day, but Gavin just laughed. He found it a hare-brained notion.

When I met him again six months later, at an airport as always, I was taken aback at his appearance. Fifty years of such a tough life were beginning to make their mark. He looked not so much tanned as weathered, his facial lines had become furrows, his movements stiff, his muscles a carapace, which made him look like one of his own crayfish. But those sea-blue eyes were the same, and to the sense of strength he always emanated was now added a touching self-assurance, the effect probably of his new financial security.

I had been apprehensive as I got ready for this meeting, youthful lightheartedness seeming no longer the note to strike. Over the years Gavin had built up an idealised picture of me, and I felt bound to live up to it. I didn't mind doing without his love for a time but I couldn't bear the thought of losing it. But once you're forty-five, everything leaves its mark on your face. A month of teaching and lectures had drained me. Well, being a race of lumberjacks they certainly knew how to drain you of your sap. The students were much more eager to learn and discuss than their French counterparts, and a lot less deferential too, both familiar and exacting, like all North Americans. You have to knock yourself out pleasing them and justifying having been brought in from so far away. Old Europe has lost that prestige which allowed it to sell itself without an effort.

With a touch of the superwoman mentality which made François tease me sometimes, I set about preparing myself as if I were competing in the Olympics. Rule 1: make sure you don't get your period during your event. I'd take the pill for six weeks without a break. Thank god for the wonders of science. Rule 2: first impressions are vital. That land of endless winter had given me a chest cold, which made me look fifty before I should. I decided to make up for it by getting my hair done the way Gavin liked, with lots of waves. His ideas of beauty were rather different from those of *Harper's Bazaar*. But my hair, already crackling with static from the dry air and central heating, couldn't survive the shock treatment administered by the local head-artists. Here, as in the States, hair salons are more like laundromats than the luxurious sanctuaries of Paris. You're washed, rinsed and dried in twenty minutes flat, guillotined by the back-to-front basins, strangled by the plastic bib, and briskly curry-combed by assistants who treat you more like a horse than a human. Then comes the moment when you're delivered up to the Great Artist, whose inspiration is liable to dry up if you're over forty. This time my groom – whom I more easily imagined as a member of the East German discus team – bluntly announced that she had never seen hair falling out like mine.

'It's autumn,' I whimpered. 'And I'm a bit tired.' 'Maybe, but this is abnormal. It's a stampede.' 'Stampede' conjured up visions of galloping baldness, sounding the death-knell for my career as a lover. A wig didn't exactly go with what the chaperone called leg-over sessions. So I agreed for my head to be soaked with a Mexican oil which smelt like lavatory cleaner, and still left my hair lifeless and dull, for all the attentions of Mario, or it might have been Emilio. Although time was short – Gavin's plane touched down in two hours – I didn't dare refuse the curling-iron or the vigorous back-combing which no one in France has practised for years, topped off by total starching with a lacquer which, this time, smelt of air freshener. Mario – or was it Emilio – casting a pitying look over my pathetically sparse locks had declared all this necessary to give my poor hair more 'body'. I tried to tell him that when I was twenty my hair had come down to my waist, like a South Sea islander's, but he just smiled politely. I've often noticed that people never believe that you were young once. They just pretend to for politeness' sake.

I fled from that temple of beauty, very late, and looking like a middle-aged doll. Luckily Gavin would notice only the doll, not the middle age. Hopefully his eyesight would have got worse, and anyway you don't see many dolls floating around at thirty degrees latitude. In the taxi I laughed with glee at the thought that in less than an hour my cormorant would open his wings to the loveliest woman in the world. Expecting one's lover does one's complexion far more good than waiting for a husband. Every turn of the taxi wheels made me more beautiful. But the Paris flight was two hours late, reducing my precarious beauty to nothing. The pitiless mirrors of the airport showed a lady with a poodle-frizz of hair, dark-ringed eyes and a faded complexion. No sign of the joy which had coursed through my veins and glowed on my skin an hour earlier!

But when Gavin appeared at last, with his air of being more solidly planted on earth than ordinary mortals, and that permanently exiled look of the sailor who has been at sea too long, I felt only a boundless tenderness. He was searching the crowd anxiously. I so flung myself on him that I cut my lip on his chipped tooth. (*'Oh-oh, cold sore in forty-eight hours, old girl!'* She'd been calling me 'old girl' since I turned forty-five.) But I didn't need to worry about mirrors or the passing years. From now on, I would see myself through Gavin's eyes. Age? What age? The age at which I was loved!

We stood there, moved, gazing at one another as if we had

both doubted we would ever meet again. Having almost given each other up, then succeeded (at the cost of acrobatic contortions for him and complex manoeuvring for me, where one false step could have wrecked the whole enterprise) in coming together again, we were as happy as a pair of children. Life had won another victory. As we waited for his luggage, we held hands like Americans, and we couldn't stop kissing in the taxi home. It was the first time we had had a home, with a kitchen, a well-stocked refrigerator, a television, a record player and a bed we would have to make ourselves. In fact we unmade it the moment we got in, to assure ourselves that the huge physical attraction was still there.

That first kiss from my guy, how often I had dreamed of it! Yes, it was still there – the power, the weakness, indissoluble.

'You remembered me, my cormorant, to return to me from such a distance?'

'I remembered you too well not to come, you mean.'

We basked in the childish but deep-seated certainty that we were where we ought to be. I stroked the curly fleece on his arms, where there were a few grey hairs now. He placed his hand on my mound, proprietorial.

'I've got the feeling that there's no way we can be cured of this sickness. I've given up hope,' I said teasingly.

'That just proves it's not a sickness. It's the opposite. It's life. You've told me often enough. I don't like hearing you talk about it as if we were sick.'

'I only meant it's like a bout of fever. Between bouts you think it's never going to return.'

'Speak for yourself. All I know is I'm done for. And that suits me fine.' He laughed his glorious, young man's laugh.

Reassured, we could move on to Act Two, 'The Return

of the Sailor'. Gavin unpacked and settled in while I delighted in doing ordinary little things all signalling 'make love to me' or 'thank you for your love'. I laid the table, brought him a whisky (he had acquired the taste in the Cape) and served up the dinner I had prepared that morning. I played at being the attentive little wife welcoming her long-lost traveller, and the accomplished flirt, with a bit of harlot thrown in. These might be the ABC of the art of love, but that's all it took to make Gavin feel he was dining with the Queen of Sheba. I savoured every look he gave me. I knew that I would never, for anyone else in the world, be the sex-bomb I was for him.

When we got to dessert, he stood and ceremoniously laid a red leather jewel case on my plate. Things were pretty serious if Gavin was giving me jewellery.

'What else could I buy for you in South Africa? Unless it's diamonds you want?' He smiled, shy and happy as I drew out a gold chain, very long and made up of heavy, even links like an anchor chain. I loved it at once.

'I'd have liked to get you something more fancy, but I didn't want to make a fool of myself. I've never managed to work out what pleases you. And I didn't want to see that face you make when I give you something you just want to chuck in the waste-paper basket . . .'

'Oh god, did it show that much?'

'You bet it did. You'd be smiling with your mouth, but that look in your eyes, it said look what the cat's brought in. I wanted to sink through the floor. It made me feel that small, and the worst thing is, I never knew where I went wrong. That handbag for instance. You couldn't have liked it. I never saw you with it, not once.'

I smiled helplessly, unable to confess that I had given it to our Spanish concierge because the orange lining nauseated me and the diamanté clasp brought me out in spots.

'I can't think why you love me with my finicky tastes and intellectual ideas, *and* what you call snobbism. Just as well I'm a sex-maniac too . . .'

'Come on, show me then. And *Karedig*, put the chain on. I want to see it on your bare skin. Next year I'll give you the anchor so you can never get away.'

I had forgotten what they were like, those first nights with a buccaneer who hadn't set eyes on a woman for months on end. What a strange gift had been made us, some first nights, so few tenth ones. I realised I had been able to leave him when I was twenty only because I had assumed I would find other lovers of his calibre. Now I know that such a love is too rare to be found twice in a lifetime.

It took us the whole of the night to calm our desire. Every murmured word, every little gesture, was what Ellen would have called pre-orgasmic. To put it more euphemistically, in the words of the romantic novelists, everything fanned our flame. I proffered him my luscious lips. He kissed them feverishly, in the words of those novelists who are scared of what goes on down below, trying to ignore the fact that sex and the brain are inextricably linked. But this story doesn't stop at the waist. Saying we made love doesn't begin to describe it properly. What brought me to ecstasy that night was Gavin's thumb in my 'tunnel', his finger on the 'button of my surcoat' and his other hand playing with my 'forehearts', while his 'rapier', his 'spear', his 'lance', swelled and reared with every discovery made by my hands and lips. These lyrical formulas of the Middle Ages I use so as not to alert my chaperone, who's becoming odious in her old age.

Should I mind that I have nothing more trendy, more

daring, more liberated to recount? Should I be sorry that we confined ourselves to what were, I admit, pretty basic practices? I know that any erotic author worth her salt would show her hero watching his partner crap, and only shoot his load – as they so nicely put it – once she's donned suspenders and black stockings or pissed in his face. These infantile exercises are supposed to produce a lordly orgasm. Well, thank you, but the plain pleasures we enjoyed were enough to bring our souls up to our lips. What's more they made me comfortable with my sexuality, freed me from that gang of evil-minded authors I thought I should admire with Sidney and his crowd. It was Gavin, unaware of their existence, who had delivered me from their loathing and contempt. He'd even delivered me from Freud, though he barely knew the man's name!

There were no winners, no losers in our endless tourneys. I could not be sure who was leading whom and, try though I might not to be the first to make demands, the slightest touch set me off again, so quickly that each accused the other of having started it.

'You're just pretending to be asleep. But I can feel that hard-on against my back, you disgusting creature!'

'What a fibber! It's you that wiggled your bum just when I was dropping off.'

We were out for the count towards dawn. I offered up silent thanks, my hand curled round his still not inconsiderable bird. As usual Gavin fell asleep in the middle of a sentence, and the sweet bird shrank. When I woke, what I held was more like a soggy chip.

All our hopes seemed to have become soggy chips in the cruel Canadian pre-winter morning light. Jet-lag had given Gavin a migraine. I had one too, must have been the vodka.

('*Nonsense*,' said the chaperone. '*These are the delights of pushing fifty. Look at all the medicines you've got on your shelf. They don't lie. Love among the analgesics, the laxatives and the hormones. And then there's that cramp you get in your calf when you're about to come. That's what old age is!*' 'Shut up, you old trout!' '*And have you noticed the way he grunts every time he gets out of a low chair! The yawning? Got stomach trouble for sure. And what about the wattles under his neck?*' 'Yeah, yeah.' '*You can yeah, yeah as much as you like. But have you looked at your arms? They're showing your age.*' 'It's not my age, it's theirs.' '*Speaking of age, your libido is becoming repugnant these days, my dear. I wonder about all these hormones they prescribe now . . .*' 'My hormone is called I LOVE YOU, YOU'RE ADORABLE. Said with such conviction that I end up believing it – of course I do!' '*Well, if he's stupid enough to find you adorable, make the best of it. You won't find another one.*' 'I'm not looking.' '*We never stop looking, dear girl. And one last detail, if you don't mind,*' she continued implacably, '*he's lost a tooth, and it wasn't in a fight like the last one! One missing tooth makes you look like a buccaneer, two and you're a grandad! You can't see it, but I can.*')

Being apart for years at a time means that you live on dreams and end up loving someone who no longer really exists, who is created out of your desire. Love by correspondence is treacherous: letters don't reveal those minor stigmas of the body which can so undermine fine sentiments. You don't belch by post. You don't put creaking joints in letters. And a man who spends his life in an all-male environment doesn't worry about hiding time's little marks of slavery.

Curiously enough I wasn't upset by the symptoms. Those marks of time on Gavin inspired nothing but tenderness in me. I was moved when he hung over me, his face convulsed with passion, his features sagging, his tongue lolling in the panting mouth. ('*The tongue of a dying turtle,*' the chaperone observed. 'Passion disfigures, everybody knows that,' I said. '*Not young men, it doesn't,*' she answered. '*And you'll have to remember in five or six years, if you're still in action, not to make love on top. The flesh sags. Or do it in the dark. As you get older, you can less and less afford to do it in broad daylight, or to walk around the room naked. And look at the way he walks: he stands up so trustingly, poor fool! He has no idea that the stuffing's gone out of his buttocks . . . He's still handsome, I grant you, but he's more of an old-timer than a juvenile lead, now.*')

Maybe. But his muscles still bulged on those thighs which sprang from his body like the branches of an oak. And I still loved the breadth of his shoulders, which the years had not stooped, and the childlike freckles on his back which, like his nature, was unbowed. I still loved half closing my eyelids, till the laughing gleam of his eyes became twin shafts of sea light. Or else to withdraw into myself, when he was in there too and concentrate on the waves of sensation which age had done nothing to diminish.

As I informed the chaperone, I couldn't have cared less that he no longer had the buttocks of a toreador. What he did have, what no toreador in the world had, was that glorious cock, the colour of old ivory, of good bread, that ever-inflating, undeflatable cock, always ready for action, smooth as a pick-axe handle polished by years of use, staunch to the last. No toreador in the world had those balls of his, round and smooth and cool, so pleasingly neat in the way they clung to his groin. At twenty I thought I wasn't made for his size. Or his pace. After my sessions with him I would be bow-legged as a jockey, my pudenda aflame. Sidney's elegant wand or Jean-Christophe's agile serpent had performed moderately well enough for me. But with Gavin, once past the first shock of penetration, I coped very well, thank you, with the size and the pace. If you haven't experienced many other people, men or women, you don't know how far love can take you. Inside us sleep unknown people, many of whom will never wake.

One advantage of being in love with a cormorant is that you can be yourself. While Lozerech had no sense of humour, or not what I called a sense of humour, he did have a sense of his own dignity, which is different. What happened was this. The friend who had lent me her apartment had a collection of old records, jazz and evergreens, and after dinner I couldn't resist nestling into my captain's arms to dance 'cheek-to-cheek', take 'a sentimental journey' with Georgia on our mind, be his 'paper doll', have him 'under my skin', and cradle our nostalgia. '*Two old fools*,' said the chaperone. Or young fools. Fools, anyway, who were lucky enough to be able to fool together.

As we danced Gavin would bring his mouth close to mine, and hold it there tantalisingly, looking at my lips as if he had never seen them before.

'It's pathological how you like kissing, Lozerech. I bet your mother left a dummy in your mouth until you were at least seven years old.'

'It's not that I like it so much, more that it gets you the way I like you.'

Mutual giggles. I tightened my arms around him. It was better not to think about the spectacle we were making of ourselves. God, supposing Loïc or Frédérique could see us now. Only my sweet François would have passed no judgement. But why worry? I was on holiday from my social image. Nothing could stop me being silly and romantic about the log fire, crackling away, the candles which I used on the table for reasons which Gavin never guessed at, or making love on the great rug of reindeer skin in the glow of the embers. Yes, I was letting myself not behave 'like my age', daring to be as I'd never be in my sophisticated circle.

I had one last lecture to give for the department of Women's Studies at the university: 'The Hidden Women of Art and History'. I knew I'd be paralysed if Gavin attended, so I tried without success to keep him away. Forbidding him to sit near the front did no good either since I soon spotted him leaning forward, his elbows on his knees, to catch every word, like a prize pupil in a Breton classroom. Nothing there of my colleagues' relaxation nor the studied casualness of the women students who made up the greater part of my audience.

In spite of myself, I chose my words with care so as not to shock him. I wanted only to alert him to the idea that women hadn't always been treated very fairly. There was no point in bringing the sex war to him. I knew already what his arguments would be, and the thought of having to listen to them made me feel sick. He was still genuinely at the Cro-Magnon stage of reasoning: say what you like, there's never been a famous woman painter or composer or scientist, that shows, and so on and so forth, while Mr Cro-Magnon eyes you to see if you've been felled with that blow from his club. Lacking the courage to face such monumental crassness, I usually steered Gavin away from these areas of contention. But now I hoped to sow just the tiniest seed of doubt in his mind.

Afterwards he was waiting for me at the exit, profoundly affected – not so much by what I had said, which had moved too quickly for him and was full of baffling concepts, but by

the applause and the approving laughter which had punctuated my lecture several times.

In fact, what moved him so was my success. Only a man
truly in love doesn't feel resentful or put down by the fact
that you're cleverer than he is.

We had to go to the inevitable little sherry party which
universities lay on after a guest lecture, but escaped as soon
as we decently could, declining all invitations. I had decided
to take Gavin to one of Montreal's star restaurants.

By one of those coincidences which happen often to lovers,
we were greeted there by an old Félix Leclerc song which
Gavin used to sing, and now sang to me in that coppery,
deep voice of his which lent dignity to any lyric.

'I can feel I'm falling for that voice all over again, like that
time at Yvonne's wedding. Remember?'

He beamed. His voice was his only vanity, and he enjoyed
using it. All around us were the wonderful smells of an
expensive restaurant – lobster, tarragon, brandy, garlic, chan-
terelles, the smells you dream about when you're alone in
winter eating luke-warm noodles. You fantasise a gourmet
dinner with the man you love, the man with whom you'll
then certainly make love, the fragrance of raspberries still on
your lips . . .

As we feasted our eyes on the menu I thought suddenly of
Marie-Josée. How unfair that she would never enjoy caviar
with a glass of ice-cold syrupy aquavit before her and the
undescribable gaze of a lover on her. How unfair that she
had never been anyone's sex-bomb, and that this man who
was legally hers felt true passion only for me, the woman
who had refused to be legally his. How many times since
their wedding had Marie-Josée reminded herself how handsome he was? Had she simply resigned herself to joining the

herd of conjugal slaves, who massage feet which step lightly off to someone else, who shampoo heads which lie on other women's pillows, who cook one-pound steaks which give their husbands the strength to make love five times a night to their mistresses? Had Gavin ever made love to Marie-Josée five times a night? What do I know? Even the most jealous eye can't penetrate the secrets of the bedroom.

These were not questions I raised with Lozerech. We spoke of Marie-Josée only when it was strictly necessary. He would have thought it poor taste to tell me what she still meant to him. When we were together we chose to forget our real lives and become two almost totally different people. I would have been embarrassed if François had met my Quebec friends who knew me only as Gavin's childish lover, holding his hand in the street and laughing at the silliest things. At Gavin's side, even my sleep had a different quality. As we grow older we tend to bury our old selves beneath the one we think is our true character. But in fact they'll all still there, just waiting for the right moment, the right gesture to bring them out into the light, pulsing with freshness and vitality.

We were living almost like a married couple, since at last, here in Montreal, I could introduce Gavin to my circle of friends. He found a niche among these Canadians who weren't so very different from him, who were still close to nature and whose language he understood instinctively even if their swear words – *tabernacle*, for instance, instead of *nom de dieu* – were a bit odd. Hearing accents even more marked than his own put him at ease. So, for once, we weren't being the furtive lovers but a couple like any other, going to the theatre or a concert, inviting friends for dinner. So husbandly did he become that one evening at the cinema – it was the first time we had ever been to a film together – he pulled the ownership trick on me.

It was the usual story: hardly had the lights gone down before the man next to me, his greying wife on his other side, went for my knee then my thigh with increasing precision. It always takes a bit of time to twig that you're being touched up deliberately, but an insistent pressure soon left me in no doubt. I crossed my legs firmly. But five minutes later he was at it, again, unobserved by the wife. I shrank into as small a space as possible while searching for some devastating riposte which, as usual, I couldn't come up with. I told myself that my silence was to spare the poor wife humiliation, and it wasn't until I was totally squashed that I got the courage to react. Picking up my bag from the floor I brought it savagely down between us on his arm, which he withdrew sharply. No further movement. Gavin hadn't noticed a thing, since he was riveted to the screen, applying himself to it as he did to everything. The film, a new Woody Allen, was ruined for me. As soon as it was over the man hurried his wife to the exit. I watched him as he fled. Colourless, ageless, not even a swine. I whispered to Gavin.

'See that man there? I'll tell you something about him when we get outside.'

I never dreamed how furious his reaction would be: he went purple with rage.

'Lucky for him he's run away, the little shit, otherwise I'd have given him a bloody lesson . . . He'd not be doing that again in a hurry, I can tell you. Little wanker! Dirty old bastard! *Kol bouet!*' Gavin thundered his way through all the insults he knew, Breton or French. He couldn't believe I hadn't immediately looked to him for protection. *I* couldn't believe that he thought himself the proprietor of my virtue.

There was no way of persuading him that it wasn't he who had been insulted, that to complain to him would have been acknowledging that I was simply an object to be quarrelled over by two jealous males. He heard me out, but his rage made him impervious to reason. I felt like a mare being rescued from a rustler by my cowboy. Poor cowboy, he thought this only proved his love for me. As so often, we gazed at each other across a yawning chasm. In the end I threw him a rope-bridge by pretending to be touched by his jealousy. But we were both upset by having such a different viewpoint. By the time we got home I was shattered and he was humiliated. It takes such a lot of time, so many different experiences, before you understand what's really right for you. In Montreal, for the first time, I was able to see Lozerech as he was in everyday life. To learn that this was a man who always held the loaf against his chest to cut it, who invariably said when I came back with the morning paper, 'I can't think why you think it's so important', then, with an attempt at witticism, 'The news won't be so new in a couple of days'; whose idea of cheering me up was to say, 'The world won't stop just 'cos I'm gone', who believed in capital punishment and thought prisons were 'the lap of luxury' – 'They should spend more time looking after old people!' This was a man whose idea of classical music was 'In a Monastery Garden' or 'Alouette' sung in close harmony in one of those Quebec nightclubs with horse brasses and hayricks stuffed with real hay, for 'atmosphere'. He was amazed that I should know 'Sombrero and Mantillas' or 'Prosper, Yop la Boum', which he'd dug out of my friend's box of 78s. Poor lamb – just because I know about Aristotle doesn't mean I don't know who Rina Ketty is. This was a man who, when I asked him about the obvious in South Africa, apartheid, say, or the diamond mines, was totally incapable of answering my questions. Sailors can somehow travel the world, all their lives, without knowing a single country. A port's a port, whether it's Singapore or Bilbao.

I wasn't always able to hide my irritation at his ignorance or his political opinions. Then he would get stubborn, silent, his eyes would darken so that I would wonder how he could continue to love me. Only some magic, some evil enchantment, held him captive. Mind you, I wasn't above doing my best to make the magic last.

(*'In short, what you really mean is shut up and fuck me,'* the chaperone started up again, determined to poison my pleasure. 'Shut it, will you?' *'The truth hurts, my girl. With you as long as you get humped . . .'*

I'm going to smash that old bag's face in, give her a proper hiding. Because, funnily enough, I don't like 'getting humped'. You can lay me, give me a good poke or pull me and tell me to get fucked, but I will not be humped! It's terms like that, not the worst ones or the most insulting, that make you see red.

'Listen, you dirty bitch, I'd like to knock the stuffing right out of you!'

She laughed incredulously. She knew I'd never managed to get rid of her. But that evening, with Gavin looking lost as our parting grew near, I was ashamed of harbouring that harmful presence of hers and at having heeded her opinions for so long. It was time to sack her. In the fire of our love, my cormorant, in your honour, I shall immolate my chaperone.)

So, for the time being, our arms round one another, we let ourselves be flayed by the desolate songs of Leonard Cohen, which were just right for our mood.

'*Karedig* . . . supposing we were married?'

'And supposing you came back to me every evening, my cormorant?'

'And supposing we woke up next to each other every day?'

In the tenderness of the moment I said things I didn't mean, or not completely. But they did us good, and what could we do but dream, since we couldn't commit ourselves to any future? Fortunately the future is never for straight away and we had learned we could live without it. We were content at the thought that Gavin would come back to Montreal the following autumn.

We didn't want to dance that evening, nor to make love. All we wanted was to be together, doing nothing at all, as if our whole life lay before us. I have no idea which of those Leonard Cohen songs lacerated us – was it 'Let's be Married One More Time' or 'I Cannot Follow You, My Love'? I only know that I was at the window, leaning against Gavin, watching the first snowflakes softly whirl beyond the glass. Our faces were close but we weren't kissing. Then, suddenly, we were floating free, out of ourselves, no longer confined by our skin, nor our sex for we were neither male nor female now. We hovered above ourselves, suspended soul to soul for an immeasurable length of time.

I remember hearing Gavin murmur, his voice unrecognisable, 'No, don't say anything . . .' but I was past speech. And what was there to be said? Each moment was an eternity.

It was the music which finally succeeded in reaching us. Then the room began to reappear. I found myself aware of a man's arm around me, his warmth, his smell, and very slowly we redescended into separate bodies and began to breathe again. We still felt infinitely fragile, frightened of speech or movement. We lay on the reindeer skin and slept, very deeply, very close. We knew that it would take at least one night of silence, one half revolution of the earth, before we would become once again distinct beings.

The last day.

We had lived so many last days I couldn't bear them any more than Gavin. It seemed that our history was made up of first days and last days, but no middle ones, which made Gavin look mortally wounded and become impotent and furious. He got more and more feverish as the hour of departure approached. In his head he was already gone twelve hours before he actually left, blind to the magazine in his hands, deaf to the record playing or the words I spoke. He told me over and over that all he had to do was shut his case and he would be ready; then informed me that he was going to shut his case, it was time to get it done, then that he had shut and locked his case and was ready. Then he sat by the door, waiting, until inevitably he stood up again and made sure the case was securely shut, tightening the strap around it as if a pack of wild beasts might rip it apart.

As I went over his features to fix them in my mind – that dear head with its tight curls, the bushy eyebrows, the curling eyelashes, the film-star mouth – I saw suddenly how tired he was looking. For a fortnight I had been too close to him to see it. The rings around his eyes had become deeper and darker as my eyes became more luminous and my skin glowed with the pleasure-hormone coursing through my veins. (Endorphine, the chaperone would say, if she was still capable of speech.) It's the man in fact, not the woman, who gives most in love-making. It's he who exhausts, drains himself, while the woman blossoms. What's more I was going back to a pleasant way of life, to a man who was waiting for me, a job which didn't tire me out, while all

Gavin could look forward to was an empty horizon, his slave-ship and the crayfish.

I only forgot that we belonged to such different species when we were making love. When I was young I imagined that love meant the complete fusion of two people, not just in the act of love or even some sort of mystic orgasm. I don't believe that now. Now it seems to me that loving implies separateness to the point of laceration. Lozerech was not, could never be, my counterpart. But that perhaps was the very basis of our passion.

11
See Montreal and Die

Age doesn't creep up on you a day at a time; but in sudden spurts. You can remain at the same stage for months, thinking that time has forgotten you, then, suddenly, you've aged ten years. For time is like a difficult adolescent, slow to settle down. One day it drops you, the next it returns with a frightening lack of consideration. You can feel terrific in the morning, and decrepit by the end of the same day. It's like growing up too in that things happen to you for the first time in your life – the first twinge in the knee when you're going upstairs, the first gum that recedes from a tooth that had been healthy until then. You've no idea when it occurred exactly, but there it is, a yellow rim between tooth and gum, a stiffness in the mornings when you get out of bed. You tell yourself you overdid it, clearing the attic the day before. But you didn't do any more than usual, it's you who are not 'as usual'. Fatigue has extended its control and will go on a little more each day. Old age is on its way.

You start by defying it. You win a battle or two, hold off the invasion with increasingly elaborate and expensive ploys, though you haven't yet reached the stage when you will spend as much time repairing the breaches as living your real life.

I was fortunate. I could contemplate my slackening body without too much anguish because I knew that someone loved it. I could pat my slightly bloated, slackening belly, because I knew that someone loved it. I didn't have to fret about the way my upper arms were sagging because someone loved them. My laughter lines, my crow's feet . . . well, I wasn't over the moon about them, but someone loved me. No deterioration could fell me as long as Gavin still desired me.

Certainly François loved me, but that was no reassurance since he never noticed any change in me. He's one of those men who want to photograph you just when you've got out of bed the wrong side, your eyes bleary, your hair a mess, your complexion particularly pale and your dressing gown shapeless – as it always is when you're over thirty or it's more than three months old. And that nice 'but you look fine to me, you're always gorgeous' means that you mistrust all his compliments, past, present or future.

Gavin wasn't nice like that, he was thunderstruck by my charms. At fifty-five he was as ardent as ever, as I was able to assure myself twice a year. Quebec had become to all intents and purposes our second country. I spent every October there, that extraordinary month of which the Québecois are so proud, with its red maples and orgy of fiery colour before the white of winter. Each autumn Gavin came for as long as he could manage, and we stole a few days in France together each spring. So ours were the equinoxes, and we were like those Nordic nixies who come to earth a few weeks each year for the mortal they love. We took what we could before retirement fixed this man of the sea in Larmor, before he became tied to an ailing wife, and put out to pasture for ever.

François knew only part of the truth. He knew that Lozerech sometimes came to Montreal, but he didn't choose to be told how much time we spent together. There was a tacit agreement that Gavin had a prior right over me, which would last as long as he lived. For our March meeting I claimed a research trip, and François pretended to believe me.

Our relationship was occasionally hurt by this, but never poisoned. I was filled with gratitude and respect for his quiet generosity in a situation where so few husbands would have been able to hide their feelings.

We prolonged our last stay in Canada by a week, to be at James Bay for the mass migration of swans and geese as they took off, abandoning a country soon to be submerged by snow for six months.

Gavin was approaching his own winter. He was fifty-seven now. His hair was grey at the temples, and the veins on his hands stood out like cords. Although his laugh no longer rang out so clearly, his powerful frame still stood square as a granite rock, braced by muscles which had never known what it was not to work, and on good days his eyes were as blue, as candid as ever.

'Let's not talk about the future,' he had begged when he arrived this time. 'I just want to make the most of every moment we've got.'

And make the most of it we certainly did. At our last meeting he had given me the anchor for my gold chain, ordered specially at the Cape, and this year he brought a locket he'd had made, engraved with our initials and a single date, 1948, followed by a dash and a blank space.

'You can get the end date engraved when the time comes.'

I nearly retorted that the time had come if he didn't say anything to Marie-Josée. Once he stopped work and we lost an alibi our love would be forced into retirement. Each night, as I fell asleep in his arms, I thought of his soon being in Brittany all the year, close to me, but completely unattainable, in bed with Marie-Josée. For the first time I was jealous of her. I stocked myself up on him as much as I could, making provision for a lean future while hoping he would soon find it unbearable to be without either his work or his love. But I had sworn not to broach the subject before the last day.

And then, too soon, it was the last day. We went through all the business with his suitcase and the strap, perhaps for the last time, and the checking of the ticket for the departure, and the time of arrival at Charles de Gaulle and the timetable of the airport link buses, so he could make it to Orly for the domestic flight for Lorient. I didn't give a damn about the time he got back to Marie-Josée for ever. He surely wasn't going to leave my life in a welter of timetables?

'Have you the vaguest idea how we are ever going to meet, now you're about to become Monsieur-et-Madame-Lozerech?'

'*Karedig*, about that, there's something I've got to tell you.'

Suddenly my cormorant looked very old, and trapped. My heart stopped.

'I went to the doctor a fortnight ago. The news isn't great.'

'Marie-Josée?' I was swept by a cowardly wave of relief.

'No, she's fine. Well, the same any road. No, it's me.'

My mouth dried. He sat down across the room from me, and spoke slowly, as if he didn't want to say what had to be said.

'I went for my annual check-up, and they did the usual cardiogram. Looks like it wasn't too good, because the doc sent me straight off to see the specialist. Dr Morvan at Concarneau. He did a whole lot of tests and . . . seems one of my arteries is completely blocked, and the other's not much better. Well, you know me. I said straight away, "Look, doc, I've got to know. What does this mean?" and he said "It's serious. We've got to do something at once. I'll take you in today for some more tests" – an angiogram or something, he said – "and then we'll decide on the treatment."'

'But when was all this? You never said anything.'

'Well, it was . . . ummm, just about a week before I was due to come here. So you can imagine I wasn't going to let anyone put me in hospital then. I said to the doc, straight I said, "Sorry doc, that's not on. There's no way I'm going into hospital today." "Tomorrow, then." "Not tomorrow, either." "What do you mean? I told you. It's serious." "Sorry doc, I've got a meeting that's every bit as serious." Well, then he said, strange like, "I'm warning you, I can't take any responsibility if you insist on leaving." That made me mad, I can tell you, and I says to him doctor or no doctor, *I* was, the one responsible for my life until further notice. "Until you've got me on a filing card in your hospital, it's my life to do what I like with." That's what I told him. He was amazed, I can tell you. He didn't like my having my own idea of what's what. "I've already told you," he says, right stuffy, "you're taking a very grave risk." "So what?" says I. "I've taken risks my whole life. No different now. Anyway, I've got plenty of life insurance. My family won't want for anything."'

Gavin seriously ill? There had to be some mistake. Such an idea had never crossed my mind. Drowning yes, but illness never. I wrestled with the inadmissible news. But he's so strong, so strong, I kept telling myself.

'It doesn't seem possible. Did you have any symptoms? Funny turns or anything?'

'I've never paid much attention to myself, you know me. People like us don't. But now you ask, yes, I did have one or two funny turns. When I bent over I sometimes felt giddy like, a buzzing in my ears. I thought it was just tiredness. A man my age, doing work like mine, it wasn't surprising. Most of my mates retired years since.'

'But why didn't you say anything when you got here? We'd have been more careful. We . . .'

'That's just it. I didn't come here to be careful. There's plenty of time for that. I didn't want to spoil it with silly worries. At least we'll have lived how we wanted to, right up to the last day and I'm not dead for all that. It's a shame in a way. Sometimes I've thought to die like that, with you, it wouldn't be a bad way to go.'

'When I think that's what you had on your mind all the time, that constant threat, and you didn't say anything!'

'I didn't have it on my mind. It's you I had on my mind, as usual. And you know I've looked death in the face a thousand times.'

As the news sank in I started to weep, in spite of myself.

'Ah, Georch, don't cry, please. It'll turn out to be nothing, you'll see. Doctors often make mistakes. I feel just the same. You haven't spotted any difference, eh?'

His face lit up with that good humour I loved so much, and I flung myself on his comforting bulk. All I wanted to do was touch him, hold him. And that was what I could never do again. Illness would deprive me of him more than ever the sea had. I sobbed against his dear heart.

'Karedig, you'll make me wish I'd never said anything. I didn't mean to tell you at first. Not a thing. I was going to write after the next lot of tests, if they decide to operate. A by-pass, that's what they call it. They open you up, change a tube or two, then you're good as new.'

'And you weren't going to say anything? Can't you see what that would have meant? You'd have been in hospital and I wouldn't have known a thing about it. I'd never have forgiven you for that, never . . .'

'That's just it, that's why I thought it was fairer to tell you.

After all, you're sort of my wife. Don't go taking it too hard. They never found a thing at any of my other check-ups for the Fisheries Board. It wouldn't be the first time they'd made a mistake, those bloody doctors. I'm not finished yet. I'm a big chap, I am . . .'

One of our ritual jokes. Well, it *was* one of our jokes, from the day it had been so hard for him to push his way into me that first time on the island at Raguenès.

'Can you credit it? They wanted to stop me flying. "If you must go, take the train," Dr Morvan kept on saying. "Might be a bit tricky, that," says I, "seeing as how I'm bound for Canada."'

'My God, if he had the faintest idea of what you were going to do in Canada he'd have thought you were mad – and that I was a murderer.'

'My life doesn't matter. What matters is you in my life. You know that. Without you, I couldn't care less what happened.'

He held me very close, as if to shelter me from the cruel truth.

'"Aris", free spar, proud Concarnois." Do you remember?'

I nodded yes. I couldn't speak for sobs. I've always cried like a small child, hiccuping.

'It does something, seeing you cry for me.' He rocked me in his arms. 'You, my George-without-an-s. My little one.'

He had never called me that before. My tears flowed faster.

'But . . . surely . . . You can't still not believe I love you?'

'I do believe it . . . But at the same time it . . . it never seemed natural to me. I was always scared one fine day you'd wake up and realise I wasn't the right bloke for you.'

'You must be mad. Do you think I could spend thirty years of my life in love with the "wrong bloke"?'

We laughed, or pretended to. The painful news was making itself felt. Sorrow lodges itself very quickly. Already I was thinking how this would turn everything upside down. How would I know if he was all right? How could he let me know if he needed me? We could both see now how precarious our situation was. That 'no' I had given him long ago in Paris was today separating us for good.

You can go for some time persuading yourself that you saved what really matters, that you retained the best part. Then comes the cruel day when the person you love isn't able to call you in his hour of greatest need. Now, I would count for less than the least of his friends. I was overwhelmed by that powerlessness which is the ultimate revenge of the lawful wife.

'I'll find a way to let you know what's happening, I promise,' Gavin assured me. 'Trust me now. I can tell you I've no intention of slinging my hook. No way.'

12
Vessels of the Heart

On 3 November Lozerech went into the hospital at Rennes for a heart by-pass.

On 5 November the surgeon pronounced the operation successful, and the patient's condition as satisfactory as could be expected.

On 7 November, without having regained consciousness, Gavin died in the intensive care unit.

'My son has passed away,' his mother told me over the telephone. It took me some seconds to work out that 'passed away' meant 'died'.

Death's sinister vocabulary, only of use just before and just after the event, was making itself heard. The deceased, the transfer of the body, the religious ceremony, the obsequies, the defunct . . . words without life, words for funeral directors to address to bereaved families, words on formal announcements. For me Gavin had not passed away. He was dead. Never again would my cormorant spread his wings.

The funeral took place in Larmor. In the little church crowded with family and friends, Marie-Josée was saying goodbye to the father of her children, Madame Lozerech to her son, and George-without-an-s was weeping for the man whom everyone believed had been her childhood friend and nothing more.

After the service I joined the long procession to the cemetery where the graves were still heaped with the chrysanthemums brought for All Saints' Day. I watched Gavin descend into the family vault to the creaking of ropes, which he had heard all his life at sea and which now accompanied him into the silence of the earth. He should have 'gone down', as he used to say, in his own element, water.

'Poor thing, he didn't get to benefit from his pension,' Yvonne kept on saying, desperate at the waste. Like her husband, her brother had contributed all his life then died before he could draw his pension. Lucky for him, I thought to myself. Cormorants can only live on the open sea; they never settle on land for long.

Gavin's eldest son had the same brown curls tipped with red as his father, that tight fleece of heavy ringlets that you see on Greek statues. I had the painful urge to run my fingers through them. He had those upturned lashes too and the same piercing blue eyes. But otherwise it was a stranger I saw, skinny and tall, with narrow shoulders and none of Gavin's robust power. As if to emphasise the difference between them, he was wearing an American blouson, casually.

They were all there, Lozerech's crew, his surviving brothers, his friends, awkward, as men are in cemeteries, caps in their hands. It was the one thing I wanted to remember him by, that seaman's cap of his, its shiny visor bent out of shape by his constantly tugging it down to wedge it on his unruly hair. An automatic gesture so familiar to me. It's little details like that which keep the dead among us: a certain way of walking, a ringing laugh, eyes which turn bashful at any talk of love . . .

I knew I would 'be miserable' without him and cry 'many a time', as he sweetly used to say. Nobody would ever call me '*Karedig*' again. But I would be left with the certainty of having received from him all that can radiate from love. And as the revolting clods of earth fell on his coffin, I suddenly wondered if, among the men I had loved, it wasn't Lozerech who had been my mate.

'He was my best son,' Madame Lozerech said over and over, dry-eyed but racked with sobs. '*Yes*,' acknowledged the chaperone, back from the grave now that death was in the air, '*he was a good person. I'm not so sure about you, but he was a good man.*'

It was raining, and the wind blew from the south-west – a sound he had heard so often. He would have wanted no other music. I touched my throat under my raincoat, feeling for the chain, the anchor and the locket on which I would not have a final date engraved. For nothing had ended. All the same I was shivering, in spite of the mild weather. As if my entire skin was in mourning for him. In mourning for a man with whom I had never once spent Christmas.

And yet, in a month's time I will spend my first Christmas without him.

Discover more about our forthcoming books through Penguin's FREE newspaper...

Penguin
Quarterly

It's packed with:

- exciting features
- author interviews
- previews & reviews
- books from your favourite films & TV series
- exclusive competitions & much, much more...

Write off for your free copy today to:
Dept JC
Penguin Books Ltd
FREEPOST
West Drayton
Middlesex
UB7 0BR
NO STAMP REQUIRED

A CHOICE OF PENGUIN FICTION

Money Martin Amis

Savage, audacious and demonically witty – a story of urban excess. 'Terribly, terminally funny: laughter in the dark, if ever I heard it' – *Guardian*

The Vision of Elena Silves Nicholas Shakespeare

'A story of love and insurrection brilliantly told' – *Sunday Times*. 'An Englishman's novel of magic realism, flavoured with the more traditional English spices such as a thriller and torchsong, and a touch of Anglo-Saxon irony … A fine literary novel … and exciting to read' – *The Times*

John Dollar Marianne Wiggins

'One of the most disturbing novels I've read in years' – *The New York Times Book Review*. 'Utterly compelling … *Robinson Crusoe* is rewritten by way of Conrad and *Lord of the Flies*, Lévi-Strauss and Freud, but with female leading roles … The result is a vision of hell that's rare in modern fiction' – *Listener*

Killshot Elmore Leonard

'I shoot people,' the Blackbird said. 'Sometimes for money, sometimes for nothing.' 'The best Elmore Leonard yet … this is naturalism carried out with a high degree of art' – *Independent*. 'A grip that seems casual at first and then tightens like a python' – *Daily Telegraph*

A Clockwork Orange Anthony Burgess

'There was me, that is Alex, and my three droogs, that is Pete, Georgie, and Dim, Dim being really dim, and we sat in the Korova Milkbar making up our rassoodocks what to do with the evening…' Horror farce? Social prophecy? Penetrating study of human choice between good and evil? *A Clockwork Orange* is, dazzlingly, all three.

A CHOICE OF PENGUIN FICTION

Stars and Bars   William Boyd

Well-dressed, quite handsome, unfailingly polite and charming, who would guess that Henderson Dores, the innocent Englishman abroad in wicked America, has a guilty secret? 'Without doubt his best book so far ... made me laugh out loud' – *The Times*

Difficulties With Girls   Kingsley Amis

Last seen in *Take a Girl Like You*, Patrick Standish and Jenny, née Bunn, are now married and up-and-coming south of the Thames. Unfortunately, like his neighbours, Patrick continues to have difficulties with girls... 'Very funny ... vintage Amis' – *Guardian*

The Levant Trilogy   Olivia Manning

The concluding trilogy of *Fortunes of War*. 'The finest fictional record of the war produced by a British writer. Her gallery of personages is huge, her scene painting superb, her pathos controlled, her humour quiet and civilized' – *Sunday Times*

July's People   Nadine Gordimer

'So flawlessly written that every one of its events seems chillingly, ominously possible' – *The New York Times Book Review*. 'This is the best novel that Miss Gordimer has ever written' – Alan Paton

The Vivisector   Patrick White

In this prodigious novel about the life and death of a great painter, Patrick White, winner of the Nobel Prize for Literature, illuminates creative experience with unique truthfulness.

Humboldt's Gift Saul Bellow

Bellow's classic story of the writer's life in America is an exuberant tale of success and failure. 'Sharp, erudite, beautifully measured … One of the most gifted chroniclers of the Western world alive today' – *The Times*

Incline Our Hearts A. N. Wilson

'An account of an eccentric childhood so moving, so private and personal, and so intensely funny that it bears inescapable comparison with that greatest of childhood novels, *David Copperfield*' – *Daily Telegraph*

The Lyre of Orpheus Robertson Davies

'The lyre of Orpheus opens the door of the underworld', wrote E. T. A. Hoffmann; and his spirit, languishing in limbo, watches over, and comments on, the efforts of the Cornish Foundation as its Trustees decide to produce an opera. 'A marvellous finale' (*Sunday Times*) to Robertson Davies's Cornish Trilogy.

The New Confessions William Boyd

The outrageous, hilarious autobiography of John James Todd, a Scotsman born in 1899 and one of the great self-appointed (and failed) geniuses of the twentieth century. 'Brilliant … a Citizen Kane of a novel' – *Daily Telegraph*

The Blue Gate of Babylon Paul Pickering

'Like Ian Fleming gone berserk, the writing is of supreme quality, the humour a taste instantly acquired' – *Mail on Sunday*. 'Brilliantly exploits the fluently headlong manner of Evelyn Waugh's early black farces' – *Sunday Times*

FOR THE BEST IN PAPERBACKS, LOOK FOR THE

A CHOICE OF PENGUIN FICTION

A Natural Curiosity Margaret Drabble

Moving effortlessly from black comedy to acute social observation, Margaret Drabble picks up the thread of the characters and stories of *The Radiant Way*, as her engrossing panorama of the way we are today shifts to the north of England. 'Confident and marvellously accomplished' – *London Review of Books*

Summer's Lease John Mortimer

'It's high summer, high comedy too, when Molly drags her amiably bickering family to a rented Tuscan villa for the hols ... With a cosy fluency of wit, Mortimer charms us into his urbane tangle of clues...' – *Mail on Sunday*. 'Superb' – Ruth Rendell

Nice Work David Lodge

'The campus novel meets the industrial novel ... compulsive reading' – David Profumo in the *Daily Telegraph*. 'A work of immense intelligence, informative, disturbing and diverting ... one of the best novelists of his generation' – Anthony Burgess in the *Observer*

S. John Updike

'John Updike's very funny satire not only pierces the occluded hocus-pocus of Lego religion which exploits the gullible and self-deluded ... but probes more deeply and seriously the inadequacies on which superstitious skulduggery battens' – *The Times*

The Counterlife Philip Roth

'Roth has now surpassed himself' – *Washington Post*. 'A breathtaking *tour de force* of wit, wisdom, ingenuity and sharply-honed malice' – *The Times*

A CHOICE OF PENGUIN FICTION

London Fields Martin Amis

'*London Fields* is more complex and affecting than its predecessor, *Money* ... It is a state-of-England novel that also examines the state of the writer ... He gives us a true story, a murder story, a love story, and a thriller bursting with humour, sex, and often dazzling language' – *Independent*

Sweet Desserts Lucy Ellmann

'A wild book ... interrupted by excerpts from cook books, authoritarian healthy-eating guides, pretentious theses on modern art, officious radio sex-advice shows, diaries, suicide notes...' – *Observer*. 'An enchanting, enchanted book' – Fay Weldon. 'Lucy Ellmann is an original' – *Guardian*

The Lost Language of Cranes David Leavitt

Owen Benjamin has a job, a wife, a son, a steady and well-ordered life, except for one small detail – Owen has spent nearly every Sunday of his married life in a gay porno movie theatre. 'An astonishingly mature and accomplished writer' – *Listener*

The Accidental Tourist Anne Tyler

How does a man addicted to routine – a man who flosses his teeth before love-making – cope with the chaos of everyday life? 'Now poignant, now funny ... Anne Tyler is brilliant' – *The New York Times Book Review*

March Violets Philip Kerr

Berlin, 1936, was full of March Violets, late converts to National Socialism. For Bernie Gunther business was booming, especially in the missing-persons field. So when Hermann Six hired him to find the murderers of his daughter and son-in-law, Gunther was glad for the variety... 'Different, distinctive and well worth your while' – *Literary Review*